THE CREED OF VIOLENCE

ALSO BY BOSTON TERAN

God Is a Bullet

Never Count Out the Dead

The Prince of Deadly Weapons

Trois Femmes

Giv: The Story of a Dog and America

THE CREED OF VIOLENCE

BOSTON TERAN

COUNTERPOINT

BERKELEY

Library of Congress Cataloging-in-Publication Data

Teran, Boston.
 The creed of violence / Boston Teran.
     p. cm.
 ISBN-13: 978-1-58243-525-1
 ISBN-10: 1-58243-525-1
 1. Fathers and sons--Fiction. 2. Illegal arms transfers--Fiction. 3. Mexican-American Border Region--Fiction 4. Mexico--History--Revolution, 1910-1920--Fiction. 5. Petroleum industry and trade--Fiction. 6. Nineteen tens--Fiction. I. Title.

 PS3570.E674C74 2009
 813'.54--dc22

                              2009025602

Cover design by Silverander Communications
Interior design by Megan Jones Design
Printed in the United States of America

COUNTERPOINT
2117 Fourth Street
Suite D
Berkeley, CA 94710

www.counterpointpress.com

Distributed by Publishers Group West

10 9 8 7 6 5 4 3 2 1

Though this is a work of fiction, certain details, backgrounds, places, and particular events are based on historical fact.

PART I

ONE

HE WAS BORN in Scabtown the day Lincoln was assassinated at Ford's Theatre. Scabtown was a parasitic hive of gaming, crib houses and red-eye across the river from Fort McKavett, Texas.

He was raised in a brothel behind Saloon Number 6. His mother was a whore, his father one of the nameless who knew her bed. The boy was nine when she died from a knife wound over money.

He took to living in a crate of wood slats he'd cobbled together under some trees near the riverbank. He carried slops and beer for pay; there was no job too menial, none too difficult. When the pestilence came he earned wages helping an army doctor with the sick and dying.

Death did not frighten him. Its heady reek meant nothing. He was much like the landscape he'd been born of, a vision hostile and burned. And of those narrow streets that are the souls of men he had seen much and learned.

He huddled alone in that tiny hut with only a ratty blanket about him. His dreams were tortuous and often sad, his childhood waylaid by reality. Most nights he was left to watching the kerosene lamps in the windows of that filthy hamlet and what stories were told there.

The boy hated his name. After his mother died he never spoke it. A prizefighter came to Fort McKavett. His face was battered, the cheeks swollen and craggy. He was not a large man, but he had enormous scarred fists and a thick back. On the parade grounds he fought a much bigger man in the baking sun. The boy watched as the fighters stalked each other round by round over that shadowless dust. It was all blood and exhaustion. But the smaller man would not be defeated and it came to be that the boy saw himself in that knotted frame, and when finally the other fighter succumbed, dropping to his knees on the blood-soaked earth, the boy experienced a place of power within himself that he could never have imagined existed. The fighter's name was Rawbone, and from that day forward it was what the boy called himself.

Not long after that he killed his first man. A drunk who'd wandered lost, after his time with a whore, down to the river darkness. He knifed the man as his own mother had been knifed and then he stole his money. The coins had blood on them and he washed them in the river till they shined.

THE ROAD OUT of Sierra Blanca followed its course through bleached and silent reaches toward the Rio Grande. From a promontory Rawbone watched an approaching island of dust rising up and away with the wind. It was 1910 and there was chaos throughout the border country of Texas.

Through the rivery heat of a white noon Rawbone began to make out details amidst the dust. It was a truck, a three-tonner. One of those new Packards, or maybe an Atlas, all bulked down and lashed with goods. The open cab was shaded by a tarp stretched across a frame supported by metal stanchions welded to the chassis. The gray tarp fluttered madly like some magic carpet. There were two men in the cab, a driver on the right and the other on the left with his boots up on the dash.

It was the one beside the driver who saw first this figure walking into the shadowless void of the road far ahead, waving a hat. He pointed.

"Now what might that be?" said the driver.

The other reached for a carbine and straddled it across his legs. They continued through the heat a long while until they came upon a raggedy, meager-looking fellow whose most prominent features were a huge forehead and tightly boned eyes.

The truck slowed and the men stared with hard vigilance as the fellow in the road called, "Please, stop." As the truck drew close Rawbone saw how its sides had been built partway up with a protective casing made from thin sheets of metal and painted in broad letters down the length of that casing on each side of the truck body were the words AMERICAN PARTHENON.

"Aye, brothers," said Rawbone as the truck finally braked. "It's Christian of you to stop. I lost my mount there in the hills." He pointed with his derby to a saddle and bridle lying by the side of the road. "I could use a ride and as for being a bummer"—he took from the inside lip of his filthy derby paper money—"I'll pay whatever it's worth to touch down in civilization."

The men in the cab glanced at each other, weighing out their reservations. The driver, a heavy, tired-looking fellow, waved him up.

RAWBONE WAS PERCHED upon the flatbed right behind the open cab. He was neither a tall man nor powerful. On the contrary, he was lean to the point of gauntness and his eyes were the color of some coming gale.

3

"So," he said, tapping his knuckles against one of the lashed crates, "what are ya carrying?"

"The makings of an icehouse to be built in El Paso that was wrongly shipped to Sierra Blanca."

From his frayed coat Rawbone took a flask and opened it. "I'll bet," he said, offering the men a drink, "when you first saw me you thought I was a breath of trouble."

The man beside the driver took the flask and drank. "We had a passing moment."

"Brothers," said Rawbone. "I've lived an unchristian life from time to time for sure. You might say I've sipped at perdition more than once." The driver drank and passed the flask back to Rawbone. "But God has seen fit to whisper a warning."

The truck slumped and rose along that pitted road into the haze of the desert slow and cumbersome while Rawbone, passing the flask again so the others might drink, listened and watched as his companions commiserated and complained about the coming revolution to the south. How with all that poverty and upheaval the Mex were now crossing the border in woeful numbers to steal jobs and insinuate themselves into the well-being of a culture that despised them. Them, with their fleshy skin and stinkin' food and brown filth and guttery lifestyle that harbored deficiencies and crime, them who meant to leech on the nation like a storm of poison.

"Well," said the driver, to all this, "God has a long memory."

Rawbone said little, preferring silence, and watching the flask go back and forth. In truth, to him, the nation meant nothing and race even less. He was the specificity of the flesh. All survive and live, and beyond that there was only death.

And yet, somewhere within this immoral selfishness there existed an outlaw place that would not die no matter how he tried to destroy it. It was like some ancient rune imprinted upon his being or a half-forgotten melody coming through the darkness.

The Mexican woman he'd married and left behind without so much as a word, the child he abandoned with one turn of a phrase. They existed yet in the sentimental mist that murdered him with quiet nightmares.

"Stop the truck," said the man beside the driver. "I'm feelin' bad."

He looked it. There was a pallor to him and a sweat ringing his temples. As the rig braked he stepped from the cab with an uncertain motion and started off carrying his carbine by its shoulder strap so it near dragged along the ground. His steps began to be dazed and then he fell and Rawbone jumped from the back and was over him before the driver could disembark.

Rawbone swept up the rifle and turned. "He's a dead man . . . and so are you, brother."

While the man lay anguishing upon the ground, something seemed to fix in the driver's mind. He blinked as if hit by revelation and looked down at the flask on the cab seat. He turned his stare to Rawbone, who had not moved, nor was he pointing the carbine. He just stood there with a steely and splayed grin as the driver, now panicking, put the truck in gear and started off.

"Aye!" shouted Rawbone at the truck. "So there you go. But you've already drunk your future down, and I can hear the trumpets playing graveside."

The truck rumbled on wildly while Rawbone slung the carbine over his shoulder then knelt and robbed the dying man of his belongings. As he lay there shuddering in the dust, Rawbone stuffed his hands down into his coat pockets. Then whistling up a tune followed off after the truck at a casual walk.

ABOUT AN HOUR further on amidst riven sandhills he saw the rig. It had veered off the road and sat canted against a stretch of rock scored by the wind.

The engine was still running as Rawbone stepped up into the open cab. The driver was alive, but barely. A trembling saliva had accumulated at the corner of his pale mouth.

"Pardon me," said Rawbone, as he leaned past him and shut off the motor. "Rest a while."

He then stepped down from the cab and, while he checked the truck for damage, noticed one of the lashed crates had come loose and cracked open beside the road.

"Ah," said Rawbone at what he saw.

He knelt over the crate. Hanging out the wood slats like the skin of a snake was a fabric feed belt mechanism for a machine gun.

He yelled back at the driver, "I didn't know they needed these to build an icehouse."

TWO

H E WAS BORN in the Segundo Barrio of El Paso on the day Ulysses S. Grant died. The barrio was blocks of squalid adobes along the Rio Grande that the city meant to raze and rebuild in good old-fashioned American brick.

He was raised in a rank alley behind a factory where desert immigrants sewed together American flags. His mother was one of those immigrants, from the state of Sinaloa. His father was a criminal and, as the boy would later learn, a murderer. The father had abandoned the family on the Fourth of July, 1893. The last he'd told his son was that he would take him by trolley to the park on Mesa Street to see the fireworks together and eat ice cream.

After this he watched the humble surface of his mother's face erode with sorrow and her grief slowly bury what God had so beautifully put there. The son took the mother by wagon to the Concordia

Cemetery and buried her in a pauper's grave he dug himself. The death left him devastated and on his own at thirteen. The desire to see his father destroyed was matched only by a string of memories born of fonder times that left an unfathomable ache across the arc of his existence.

The boy took to living on the roof of the factory where those at work on the sewing machines did double shifts stitching together flags. He was a day laborer in the Santa Fe Railroad yard that shouldered up to the barrio. It was brutal work that drove men into the earth like paltry nails. Yet he had not only the fury to survive but the faith of mind to flourish.

He wore around his neck a tiny gold cross with one broken beam that had been his mother's. It was not some holy trinket or talisman but every wistful and nostalgic wish that had ever been.

He could read and write, and his father had taught him the creed of weapons. He was unafraid of death, understanding it was only the seamless moment that takes you to somewhere else.

He was not a tall young man; rather he was thin and muscled with a huge forehead and shaded eyes. His hair was black and straight, his skin tawny, his features refined.

His name was, for him, rife with shame, and after his mother's death he changed it. She had always dreamed of a pilgrimage to Lourdes, where the Virgin Mary appeared to the child Bernadette Soubirous, and ever afterward, when asked, he said his name was John Lourdes.

He started as an oil boy in the roundhouses. He rose in the ranks to run a yard gang. He spoke two languages fluently, and having been weaned by a criminal, had an intuitive feel for the devilry within men. He was moved to security, and soon after promoted to railroad detective.

In 1908 Attorney General Charles Bonaparte organized the Bureau of Investigation with its own staff of federal law enforcement officers.

John Lourdes was invited to join. And so, at the age of twenty-three, he became a special agent working for the federal government in El Paso, Texas.

HE LEANED AGAINST the rail fence that flanked the Rio Grande by the Santa Fe Bridge. He had a week's worth of beard and clothes that cried out with wear; even his slouch hat had shear lines along the creases. John Lourdes was an unemployed rough killing time and cigarettes alongside a row of other roughs trying to scratch up day work at an employment shed. At least that's how he wanted to come across so as not to draw attention to himself, while day after day he watched the foot traffic pass through customs between El Paso and Juárez.

The Mexican Revolution had begun in 1910 when President Porfirio Díaz promised free elections, then proceeded to deny them. This act was the pebble that presaged the avalanche. Mexico was decaying under the forces of exploitation, poverty and foreign interests. One thousand people controlled the vast majority of the nation's wealth. Illiteracy, child mortality and peonage became the sires of violence.

El Paso and its sister city, Juárez, were the epicenter for revolutionaries, expatriated nationals, would-be saboteurs, two-dollar-a-day undercover agents working for both sides, con men, corrupt Rangers and an assortment of human flotsam who carried illegal fires in their hearts.

John Lourdes had grown a mustache that was sleek and modern, to fit the times. He ran a finger across his upper lip as he studied the foot traffic. He possessed the intangibles of discipline and patience as well as an eye for the particulars of people. A look or gesture often exposed a hole right into them. He followed anyone who aroused suspicion and he scratched out every detail in pencil in a pocket notepad.

His father had asked him once as a boy, "Do you want to know what people are really like?"

They had been in Juárez at an open-air market overrun with shoppers. His father pointed from face to face, then knelt down, pulling his son close. There was always a bit of fever in his father's voice when he was excited. "Do you want to know how? So you can never be tricked nor fooled?" The boy's eyes widened. "So no one can ever make a game of you. Nor spin you, nor straight edge you. Like that," he said snapping his fingers, "you can know. Do you want to know? Do you want to know how?"

The boy nodded because he saw his father so needed him to want to know.

"Well," he whispered to his son, "be indifferent to every man . . . and you will know."

That moment, in all its profound self-interest, wrapped around him like a strangle cord as a young girl walked past, just a shadow reach away, and crossed back to Juárez. It was the third time in as many days he'd noted her.

And it wasn't because she was young and lovely in a rather simple and unassuming way. She couldn't have been more than sixteen or so at the outside, yet there was this calming silence she emanated as she pressed on about her business, that was in direct contrast to the nervous and wary pen stroke of her eyes as she watched and weighed every action before her.

The first time he'd seen her, she was in the waiting line for the quarantine shed just below the bridge. The building was wind-beaten brick with a long, fluted chimney, and there Mexicans crossing to the United States went to be stripped down and deloused.

It was a horrible and humiliating experience. His own mother had suffered it upon crossing. He'd overheard her once with other women, their voices cloaked, how they'd been stripped and left to stand in waiting lines on a cement floor to undergo medical inspection, while the workmen spared no one with their eyes.

Since becoming a federal agent he'd been in that building often when hunting criminals. He'd seen how they used pesticides and gasoline, and sometimes a form of sulfuric acid for the delousing. The clothes too were fumigated, then put in huge steam dryers, which sometimes melted shoes. The place was nicknamed . . . the gas chamber.

The girl walked past afterward and on into a dusty procession of humanity up Santa Fe, and he saw how everything her eyes touched produced this ripple of uncertainty across her features. The next day he saw her again coming out of the quarantine shed. She passed by, only to return an hour later.

The third day the process was repeated. But by the time she returned he'd been enlisted in conversation by two German designers. They'd gotten permission to go into the quarantine shed. They'd done draftmen's sketches of its interior and they were asking John Lourdes if it was true the government weeded out the deformed and the deviant, as they too had, in their own country, problems with what they described as "the unclean," that needed to be dealt with.

If they'd understood Spanish, what John Lourdes said in reply as he started toward the bridge could not have been confused as an answer.

HE FOLLOWED HER down the Avenida Paseo de Triunfo. There was a black mood about the streets. Wall graffiti insulted the regime; groups of men stood in heated conversation. Young boys carrying rifles in a primitive street militia marched past the Monument to the Fighting Bulls and, holding their weapon muzzles high and cursing El Presidente, fired into the air.

Heads turned. Birds slanted skyward down the length of the Paseo. Only from the girl was there no reaction as she walked on. It was then John Lourdes understood her calm silence and those wary stares—she was deaf.

Next to a movie theatre was a two-story office building the girl entered. A shop on the first floor had a sign in the window: TRAVEL MEXICO. Out front were a couple of Maytag Touring Cars that had painted on the side: WE'LL TAKE YOU ANYWHERE THE WIND CAN GO!

He followed her into the building. The hall was dark and filthy. He could hear her footsteps on the stairs. On the second floor she went into an office. He reached the landing as the door closed. He walked past cautiously. He could hear voices through the open transom and see light angling down a far wall from a skylight. He looked to one end of the hall and then the other, where there was a stairway to the roof.

On the roof he walked a row of skylights; most were poled open to let the dead air escape the paltry offices. When he reached the one instinct said was it, he took off his hat and squatted down near the opening, but far back enough not to be seen. He could just make out the girl in a picture frame of light.

With head downcast, she stood alone. There were cloudy voices, men speaking English and Spanish. A door opened and closed. A shadow climbed the wall. A man spoke. He had a gritty voice. John Lourdes could not see his face, only his trouser legs and mountain boots. An arm stretched out holding a blanket, and the girl began to undress.

Her clothes slipped to the floor. The blanket was tossed to her. She wrapped it around herself, while averting her eyes from the man. He knelt down and scooped up the clothes and left.

THREE

RAWBONE HAD A decision to make as he sat in the idling truck forty miles east of Fort Bliss. Primal simplicity would dictate he forget El Paso. Best he swing south to Socorro or Zaragaza, then stake his way north to Juárez. People on the verge of a bloodletting will always pay top dollar for weapons and a truck. He had enough gasoline to make the journey and he'd robbed both men before he burned their bodies.

He smoked as he looked out toward the bladed hills that preceded El Paso. On that day in the year of our Lord, Rawbone was forty-five years old. On the truck seat was a photo he'd taken from the driver's wallet. He and his wife were posed on the platform of the Stanton Street Depot with their blank-faced kids.

He knew the depot well from that other life. He'd met his wife just blocks away on the Lerdo Tramway. Mules pulling the streetcar in the rain. Her voice like candlesmoke when he asked could he sit beside her. He swore his youth belonged to someone else, not him. Though he closed his eyes, the stillness of distance did nothing to strip the past away. It was there yet, forsaken but not forgotten.

There had been a city attorney in El Paso. A more corrupt or kinder man he'd never known. Wadsworth Burr would tell Rawbone, "Things happen that cannot be explained by any laws we know and they carry the damn secret with them all the way to our oblivion."

RAWBONE DROVE TO the barrio he'd known when married, only to find it gone. In the oppressive heat he walked a block of brick storefronts that had once been the adobes he frequented. The alley where they had lived was now a routeway for telephone poles cluttered with wire. His wife had been dead years, this much he knew. His son . . . was a ghost.

He lit a cigarette and surveyed what once had been. On the corner of the alley where the sewing factory had stood was now a pawnshop; opposite was a gun seller where in one window was an ad that featured Bat Masterson with a Savage .32 automatic . . . the ten-shot quickie . . . A TENDERFOOT, read the ad, WITH A SAVAGE COULD RUN THE WORST SHARPSHOOTER IN THE WEST RIGHT OFF THE RANGE. In the other shop window was another advertisement. This depicted a woman in bedclothes aiming a Savage at the viewer: THE BANISHER OF BURGLAR FEAR . . .

The barrio hadn't changed, he thought, it's only been dry fuckin' cleaned.

OVERLOOKING DOWNTOWN WAS the Satterthwaite Addition. There was a dreamy tranquility to those manicured estates as the sun fell away beyond the far mountains. Wadsworth Burr lived in a huge Mission-style house near the corner of Yandell and Corto.

Rawbone was shown to the den by a young Oriental girl, who moved with an airy silence over the tiled floor. The high ceiling kept the rooms cool just as he remembered.

Burr sat at a campaign desk before a grand bay window from where one could see the Rio Grande wend its way through a withering sweep of desert.

Burr was not much older than Rawbone, but to see this once-noted attorney now was a study in startling contrasts. He had just begun the morphine shortly before that July Fourth Rawbone abandoned his family.

"You look like something straight out of Dickens, or at the very least, Hugo," said Burr.

"I'm in dire need, if that's what you're saying."

Burr motioned toward a serving cart with its chorus line of liquors. Rawbone tossed his derby aside. As he poured he saw Burr's wrists were mere belt widths and his scooped-out cheeks and boned-down jaw more likely features you'd see on a slumworn tramp.

Rawbone took a drink. Passing around the desk, he shook Burr's hand and noticed a hypodermic waiting on a white dinner napkin.

"You should have stuck to whiskey."

"But I had such an overwhelming need to express my character flaws."

As Rawbone walked over to the window, Burr asked, "What brought you out of exile?"

"I stumbled upon a business opportunity."

"Ahhh. I'll curb my curiosity."

Rawbone kept looking out the window as the earth began to tint under dusk. "I see the Addition is called Sunset Hills now."

"Yes . . . it has a certain cemeterial ring, doesn't it? It seemed Mr. Satterthwaite suffered a reversal of fortune, which is something, I think, you should particularly note."

Burr reached for a sheet of letter paper and an ink pen.

"I see you still prefer them Chinese," said Rawbone.

Burr wrote something on the sheet of paper, folded it, then set it like a pup tent on his desk. "There has always been a place in my heart for deviance and passivity."

"I walked the barrio. Adobe Row is gone."

"It was a reasonable eventuality. All cultures prefer to replace someone else's vanities with their own."

Rawbone came around the desk again. He took from his pocket a bill of lading and handed it to Burr. "It's from an import-export shipper here in El Paso. What do you know of it?"

Burr studied the piece of paper. "I don't know the company. But I see these are items for building an icehouse." He handed it back. "You and the makings for refrigeration tests the limits of the imagination."

"There's a revolution coming," said Rawbone.

"It's here."

"Weapons will sell for a premium. As will three-ton trucks."

"Leave the city tonight," said Burr. "Go to Juárez. I'll arrange introductions to some very private people."

Rawbone's attention seemed to have drifted momentarily. "What do you know about the boy?"

Burr studied his friend carefully. "He wouldn't be a boy now, would he?"

"Is he here?"

Burr pointed to the paper tent on his desk. Rawbone took it up between two fingers and read: *What can't be forgotten, must remain forgotten.* Rawbone then folded and refolded the paper and put it in a coat pocket.

"You can take up in the apartment above the garage. I have plenty of clothes. Some will fit you. Look the part."

"Thanks, Wadsworth."

He poured another glass and reached for his derby. As he started out Burr, upon reflection, said, "Consider your options but don't get lured into some lost cause." Rawbone stopped partway across the room and looked back. "You were always at your best," said Burr, "when you were selfish and remorseless, with just a hint of humor."

"I'll note it, friend."

"Note it well. The city is not like it was. There's violence at hand. Undercover agents everywhere. More sheriffs, more law enforcement, more Rangers. And now the Bureau of Investigation."

"It's good to know we're in such efficient hands."

"There's a new law . . . the Mann Act. It gives the BOI a wide latitude when it comes to national security investigations. They have offices in the Angelus Hotel. And you know who's in charge . . . Justice Knox."

FOUR

THERE WAS A phone in the theatre next to the building where the girl was. John Lourdes called the BOI office at the Angelus Hotel. His field commander, Justice Knox, was out, but an operative wrote down Lourdes's observations and requests.

The girl remained overnight. She slept on a flimsy sofa bundled up like a child. A single candle burned on a table nearby. Shadows bore out the window in that room was barred.

John Lourdes took up on the stairwell at the end of the hall so he could watch any comings and goings from that office, but there were none. He balled up his coat to use as a pillow and played the role of bum stealing a place to sleep off the street. The building grew dark and empty. Any vague and distant sound was like the fleeting tone of dreams.

As he waited for daylight to continue his surveillance, he could not get the girl out of his mind. She seemed to touch certain inarticulates within him. He also found that she and the conversation with the Germans, if you could call it that, seemed entwined, as if they were part of one single experience.

He had always been at his investigative best when details were studied at a distance. He was at his most comfortable with the world when that too was experienced at a distance.

He approached what he was experiencing with the same cool eye. As for the girl, it was in great part her silence that affected him. The silence she exuded as she crossed that bridge and walked alone almost otherworldly from all that was going on around her, while at the same time being intensely on guard.

Now, the Germans and their comments about the "unclean" left him trussed up with his past openly exposed. What they said had infuriated him not only for its degrading and racist implications but because he, in fact, felt in some way "unclean."

Neither the BOI nor Justice Knox had any idea the criminal and murderer called Rawbone was his father. He'd relegated that detail of his heritage to the trash heap of history, inventing a story about an Anglo father, now deceased, named Lourdes. John Lourdes had done so not only because he felt unquestioned shame, but because he was also driven by aspirations of career and betterment and knew this crime of chance would not play to his favor.

That was the term a friend of his father's used, a man his mother thought to be "unholy and unsavory." The friend was a disgraced attorney named Burr. As a boy he'd been to the great white house in the hills above El Paso with his father. Often it was at night, often the men spoke in secret, often afterward his father would disappear for days at a time.

One night, before leaving, Burr had slipped some paper money into the boy's shirt and told him, "See your father there? You can thank him; your birth is a crime of chance . . . but all birth is a crime of chance."

Burr's manner was such that even the very young John Lourdes knew the statement was meant in a malicious way to taint him. And now, all these years later, beyond the restless hours and mysteries that afflicted him, beyond all aims, objectives and intentions there was this need as final as final could ever hope to be, that he, John Lourdes, would be the one to bring about his father's bloodletting, that he would be the cause hand behind his death.

As DAWN BEGAN to seep across the building doorway, there came the sound of distant and sporadic gunfire. It was not a good sign. Not much later the girl came out of the office with a man. He must have been in there all night because John Lourdes had not seen him enter. He was a small fellow, bespectacled and Mexican. He was neatly dressed and rather unassuming except for the knife sheath hanging from a pistol belt under his green felt coat.

They made straight for the Santa Fe bridge with Lourdes following, but this was no ordinary morning. The street was spilling over with people. Pamphlets were being passed out urging the citizenry to take up arms against the Díaz government. There was a rabble atmosphere of anger and retribution for the overturning of free elections. Making it through the chaotic foot traffic was near impossible. Everywhere weapons were being brandished and fired off with wanton disregard. A government flag was burned in the street, its smoking ashes singeing the air. Up ahead, at the hipódromo, the racehorses had been loosed from their stables and were being stampeded down the Paseo.

It was then President Díaz's mounted shock troops appeared far up the Paseo, their columns re-forming to become a phalanx across the boulevard. When the commander ordered lances readied, his troops answered crisply.

They held there with the sun to their backs, and their battle line shimmered in the heat. The commander demanded the crowd disperse,

21

but it remained defiant. The Mexican with the girl in tow shouldered his way through the shouting insurrectos toward what he assumed was the safety of the sidewalk buildings. Again the commander shouted his orders and again the crowd answered in a fanfare of epithets and arms held aloft with clenched fists.

The command was given, the surge of troops immediate and brutal. Most of the citizenry fell back in a panic; some stood their ground and fired. The street became a pall of yellow dust and screams. The ensuing pandemonium swept over the Mexican and the girl. They were lost to each other. He was taken in a wave of humanity down the sidewalk while she was trampled over.

John Lourdes managed to hold ground then shoulder his way forward. He reached the girl, who lay on the sidewalk trying to protect herself. He pulled her up and into a doorway. She was bloody and frightened; she was trembling. He held her by the arms till she calmed. She thanked him with a nod and by putting a hand on his heart. His thought: Get her back across the border and somehow question her. Suddenly the Mexican punched his way through a wild frieze of bodies in headlong retreat. He had a revolver drawn and pointed. He threatened John Lourdes in no uncertain terms to be away, now, be away.

THE SOUND OF gunfire was evident as far as the Rio Grande. Word quickly spread about the noonday assault at the hipódromo. Americans gathered along the riverbank. The air above the buildings along the Avenida Paseo de Triunfo was heavy with smoke. By the time the Mexican herded the girl to the bridge, John Lourdes was there waiting.

He watched her descend the weathered planking to the quarantine shed. The Mexican kept her under steady surveillance until she disappeared within that grim-faced building. He then looked over to the American side and seemed to acknowledge someone. John Lourdes scanned the crowd along the river to see who it might be.

The girl appeared, then as usual started up Santa Fe. John Lourdes set off to follow. She hadn't gone but a few yards when a man slipped through the crowd and took hold of her arm.

He was very tall and quite lean. He was much older and wore pleated pants and a vest. He had a long, dour face and said nothing to the girl.

A trolley slowed and the man pressed the girl to board. John Lourdes swung toward the rear steps, and as the girl was being led to a seat, she noticed him. She stared so that the man with her turned to find out what had caught her attention. John Lourdes eased back into a faceless wall of passengers. They rode the line as far as the park at Oregon and Mesa. They entered the Mills Building. John Lourdes followed them and others into the elevator. The girl made sure not to look at him. She was trembling so. They took the grated elevator to the fifth floor. They went in one direction down the hallway, John Lourdes the other. The office they entered was numbered 509. The downstairs directory read: SIMIC SHIPPING — IMPORTS AND EXPORTS, ROOM 509.

There was a tobacconist in the lobby beside the entrance to the Modern Café. It was from there John Lourdes called in. Just across the park was the Hotel Angelus, which headquartered the BOI. John Lourdes was told Justice Knox and an operative were on their way from northern El Paso. He bought cigarettes and waited by the Café doors. He detailed everything in his pocket notebook.

He was slipping the notebook back into his coat pocket and starting outside for a touch of sunlight and air when he walked right into a gentleman entering the lobby. John Lourdes looked up to excuse himself but could only stare.

"Now looking down as you walk along may score you a lot of loose change," said the man, "but you've got to keep those gunsights at eye level if you really mean to make something of yourself."

And with that his father offered an offhanded grin, then was on his way.

FIVE

RAWBONE SAUNTERED INTO the Simic Import And Export offices. A half-dozen men were grouped in private conversation around a desk. They grew silent with his entry. He stood there waiting in his tailored suit and crisp derby.

"May we help you in some way?" said the one sitting at the desk.

"It's the right question, for sure," said Rawbone, "but the wrong man is asking it."

He approached the desk and handed over the bill of lading from the truck. The man studied it with quiet regard as the others looked over his shoulder. His expression tightened further as he glanced up at Rawbone. He stood and walked to a door to a private office and knocked. "Mr. Simic," he said. "I need a moment."

The door opened slightly and the man entered. Through the opening Rawbone glimpsed a young girl wrapped in a blanket sitting in the corner on the floor.

While he waited, Rawbone sat back on the wood railing that demarked the office entry. He took on the men's stares by disinterestedly fanning himself with the derby.

The inner office door opened and the man from the desk came out first. He was followed by an older gentleman with a long and dour face, who held the bill of lading. He did not bother to introduce himself.

"How did you get this?" he asked.

Rawbone gave no answer.

"The drivers?"

Rawbone crossed himself.

The men in the room took on the mood of a hunting party. Simic instructed one of the men to lock the door. As he did Rawbone opened his suit coat and reached for a handkerchief that happened to be in the same pocket where the black handle of an automatic protruded for anyone to see.

"Who are you?" Simic asked.

"Think of me," said Rawbone, "as . . . Tom, the bootblack. Ah, you're not familiar . . . Horatio Alger's hero, educated at the hard school of poverty. Who with a smile and good cheer overcomes the hardships of existence to acquire . . . a comfortable fortune." His grin of sarcasm disappeared. "Now, let's put our cards and our pure hearts on the table."

JOHN LOURDES CROSSED the street in front of the Mills Building. On that day in the year of our Lord, he was twenty-five years old. He stood under the shade of a great elder at the entrance to San Jacinto Park from where he could watch the lobby and wait on Justice Knox. That reviled gusano of a father had walked right out of the scarred regions of memory and straight into the daylight, all suited up like a gent and with the cool arrogance of one who believes himself beyond the trappings of right and order.

But today, there would be a reckoning.

Then something, call it superstition if you will, took hold of John Lourdes. He glanced back into the park down a shadowy walkway. He had come here many times as a boy with his father. There was a pond with a stone wall around it where lived half a dozen alligators. How they'd come to be there was uncertain. But one winter night his father had persuaded a few drunken wilds to go down to the park and sack up those creatures and get them out of the cold to keep them from freezing.

So there he'd been watching as his father and a band of drunks wrestled one prehistoric monstrosity after another into canvas gunnies. They carried them back to that dingy saloon and kept them warm by the stove while the boy sat on the bar cross-legged and watched his old man resting in a chair amongst them. He had a cigarette in one hand and with the other flicked mescal from a bottle onto each sacked gator.

"I baptize you," he said, "in the name of the father and the son . . ."

John Lourdes needed to remember, nothing was beyond his father's unpredictability.

Justice Knox arrived with another agent named Howell. Knox was a plain, soft-spoken man. He had poor vision and wore spectacles and was singularly obsessed with the security represented by the bureaucracy. His core belief: People's central need and desire was for bureaucracy, not freedom, not rebellion, not individuality. Man longed for effective bureaucracy, and its ultimate expression was order.

Knox was never swayed by anger or revenge. He was in that respect heartless, and it made him, in turn, beyond the reach of sympathy or compassion. He had no personal attachment to his agents, no interest in their private welfare, and he demanded their attitude toward the job be precisely the same as his.

"The girl?" he asked.

"She's still up in 509."

Knox put his hands on his hips and looked at the building, and while he considered a plan John Lourdes gathered himself and said, "Sir, there's something else—"

WHEN RAWBONE LEFT the Mills Building he crossed the street and cut straight through San Jacinto Park. His hands were in his pant pockets and he wore the derby at a cocky angle. Yet he was wary enough to keep glancing back.

At the pond tourists leaned their kids over the stone wall to see the alligators moving through the still and mosquito-laden waters. He was not much beyond it when the memory of a winter night back in '92 washed over him. He could see the boy there in that grimy saloon, the kerosene lamp above him curtained with smoke. His son . . . he'd just turned seven.

There was no time now; the present had the upper hand. He jumped a trolley. He rode it half a dozen blocks till he came to an empty lot where he'd parked Burr's Cadillac. He geared it up and gunned it and said goodbye to downtown in a sweep of dust.

Rawbone drank and loosed his tie as he explained to Burr his hour with that jury of strangers in the fifth-floor office. One thing Burr would swear to about his friend, he could elevate a simple act of criminality into a moment of personal splendor.

He told Burr he was jacking it out of El Paso that night. Then, as he toasted the air and said, "Mexico or bust," Burr saw him hesitate, saw those agate eyes pare away everything around him except the half-caught sound of tires breaking in front of the house, then the scruff cutting of boots across gravel. He had the curtain open quick and saw

Justice Knox and two men sprinting up the walkway and spreading around the house with weapons drawn.

"Goddamn," he said, scrambling across the den past Burr and through the kitchen, frightening the cook so she gasped, only to be met by gunfire as he made the screened-in porch.

He dropped down to the floor, gun drawn, and huddled up behind the porch wall. He sat there out of breath, and as he was ordered to surrender he yelled back, "You're either good Christians or bad shots. Either way it doesn't speak well of you."

Then Rawbone heard scattershot voices moving through the house. He could make out Justice Knox shouting to his men, who answered they had him pinned down on the porch. He pulled his legs up and rested his arms on his knees.

Justice Knox called to him from rooms away, "Give it up peacefully!"

Rawbone banged the back of his head against the porch wall in anger. "I'm up some well-digger's ass who's at the bottom of a hole." He shouted, "What says my attorney?"

"Give it up peacefully," Burr answered.

"Is that your best legal advice?"

"I'm saving that for later. So take heed."

He rose up in the sandy light, arms first, and was surrounded there on the porch steps. John Lourdes watched how he took his capture as a boring and peremptory ceremony. And as they manhandled and cuffed him, Rawbone noticed one of the agents was the young man he'd spoken to in the building lobby. "Well," he said, "I see you took my advice and got those gunsights up."

SIX

IT HAD HAPPENED too fast and not near with the force John Lourdes had always imagined. He'd hoped some physical law of existence would be affected. There had been no suffering and no acknowledgment from that dusky figure that he would now face his end. John Lourdes felt barren and empty, as if the dust of everything that had been his life blew through the whetted bones of his chest.

John Lourdes rode with Justice Knox and another agent in a poor excuse for a touring car. Agent Howell had been ordered to follow the girl from the Mills Building and stop her at the border. She was now being held incommunicado in a basement room at Immigration.

When Knox and his agents arrived, the girl was bundled up on the floor behind some filing cabinets. She was a pathetic sight rocking back and forth while keeping her face hidden behind her hands.

"What's going on here?" asked Knox.

Howell pointed at the girl, "She's an imbecile."

Lourdes walked past the agent, saying, "I told you she was deaf."

"She may be deaf, but she's an imbecile."

Knox rebuked Howell with a look. "She has information we need."

"She's an imbecile."

Lourdes knelt down. The girl clenched up at being touched, but by proceeding gently he managed to get her hands away from her face. When she finally saw who it was, she seemed to ease a bit, even as she stared at the strange men in this hostile setting. He coaxed her to stand and then to sit at a table. The room had brick walls and no windows. There was a single electric light that hung from the ceiling. It was a dire kind of place, unlikely to put one's fears at rest, but he tried by placing a hand to his heart and then touching her shoulder.

He turned to his commanding officer. "Sir?"

"Does anyone have an idea how we deal with her?"

No one did. Only John Lourdes offered, "May I try something, sir?"

"She seems to be at ease with you."

He sat at the table opposite her. He had been turning over in his head ways to try and reach her during the ride to Immigration. He took out his pocket notepad and pencil. He began to write.

"She's an imbecile," said Howell.

Lourdes did not answer that.

"And besides, she's Mex."

"I'm writing in Spanish."

"Oh," said Howell. "I forgot. You're one of them."

Lourdes turned and looked up at Howell. "That's enough," said Justice Knox.

When he was done, John Lourdes passed the notepad across the table to the girl and pointed to what he'd written: Can you read—write? Do you understand?

She stared at the note, at the men, then she just sat there within the confines of a complete sadness. I understand you, he thought, I'm as alone here as you are. The men were getting restless. John Lourdes took the notebook and wrote: *Be not afraid. God and I will see to your welfare.*

He passed her the notebook again. She looked at it, then at him with the naked honesty of a child. She took the pencil and began to write, line after line, and when she was done John Lourdes read aloud: Yes, I can read and write. I am much better in Spanish than English. But I can do both. I was not born deaf. That happened when I was ten. Before that I went to the nun's school at Our Lady's Church.

John Lourdes asked the commander, "What now, sir?"

"Ask why she was going back and forth across the border."

She watched as he wrote, and then wrote back: *Will I be in trouble?*

He wrote: *No.*

She wrote: *I was carrying money stitched into my clothes.*

He read that aloud. The agents looked and talked amongst themselves. The commander instructed John Lourdes, "Ask what the money was for."

She answered: *My father ordered me to do it. So I did it.*

Lourdes wondered and wrote: *The man who brought you to the border, the one with the revolver. Who is he?*

She wrote with trepidation: *He . . . is my father.* She added: *What will happen to me now? My father saw me taken. He will demand to know. I will have to explain. I am afraid.*

John Lourdes looked at Justice Knox, who spoke. He was sober and deliberative. "Money coming from the south. It certainly is not narcotics. Contraband . . . weapons. That's most likely. So we possibly have linkage to a smuggling operation. How deep does it run here and across the border? What political ramifications does it have? We don't want to disrupt them till we know more. That means the girl has to go back. Otherwise they might assume the worst and restructure their operation."

"Threaten the man through his daughter," said Howell. "Jail her. Give her a few days in the pit, then bring the father here."

"That's a three-wheeled idea, sir," said Lourdes. "The father might be nothing more than a pair of boots."

Justice Knox removed his glasses. He rubbed at the pinch marks on his nose. He asked one of his agents about the immigration statutes.

"There are restrictions, sir, against the morally suspect, the diseased, those engaged in contract labor—"

"The LPC provision," said John Lourdes, "that would make the most sense."

"Yes," said the agent, "the-likely-to-become-a-public-charge statute. It would, sir, make sense in her case."

Knox, after some consideration, concurred. "Have Immigration write her up for an LPC. Lourdes, explain it to her, then have her released."

Later, he requested permission to make sure the girl got safely across the border. Knox agreed, and so John Lourdes drove her to the nun's school at the church. He advised her to go there and have one of the nuns escort her home, believing it would lend validity to the LPC charge and assuage any fears or suspicions her father might have as to why she'd been picked up and interrogated by Immigration.

As they sat in front of the church, where the smoky light from the sacristy cast a warm gold upon the night, Justice Knox received a phone call at his office from Burr. He wanted to meet, that evening if possible, to negotiate a deal for his client with the BOI, offering in exchange relevant information about a smuggling operation.

The girl pointed to John Lourdes's pocket for his notepad and pencil. She wrote: *I don't even know your name.*

He wrote: *John Lourdes. I know yours—Teresa. It is a lovely name.*

She drew on a new page a simple cross with lines from it fanning out. He pitched up his arms and shoulders as if to ask what this means.

She wrote beneath the cross: *God will shine down on you when you are most in need.*

He thanked her and slipped the pad into his pocket. He sat with a far-off stare and when he finally turned to her, she looked away. She'd been looking at him too long and too intensely and when she realized it, she became self-conscious.

He suddenly had this feeling of boyhood, of who he'd been before . . . the fall of angels, so to speak. The feeling was all around him in the scented dark, in the light from the church doorway, on the dry sage breeze. And above all, in the simple portraiture of that young girl with hands folded across her lap.

The pure aesthetic of being truly alive and filled with possibility possessed him. He closed his eyes and tried to completely absorb the feeling and so hold on to it. Then she touched his arm to say she was getting out of the car.

He tried to sleep that night, but he could not. He lay in bed in the tiny room he rented that was his whole world. This day in 1910 had washed upon the opposing shores of his existence, and while he lay there a deal was being exacted that would cast him upon the shores of yet another existence.

In the morning he was awakened by his landlord. There was a call on the hall phone. Justice Knox ordered him to come immediately to the courthouse, and to speak with no one. Rawbone was going to be released.

SEVEN

THE DOWNTOWN COURTHOUSE was an ornate three-story edifice that stood out grimly against the Spartan timelessness of the west.

There was no official federal courthouse; the U.S. court and federal offices were housed on the second floor. The building had a dome, and light from that dome spilled down through a ceiling well.

Justice Knox was in conversation with an attorney when John Lourdes arrived. He waited impatiently, the coming sunlight from the dome hot against his neck until the conversation was done. Knox, alone, approached him.

"Mr. Lourdes. I appreciate your promptness. We have a lot to—"

"Sir. Am I to understand that—"

"Mr. Lourdes, you will understand when I am done explaining. And then you will have no need to jump-start my conversation."

"My apologies, sir."

Knox took him by the arm and they paced off a few steps. Knox spoke privately about the previous night. The district judge had given Knox use of his private office so as few people as possible would know about the meeting. Knox had sat behind the judge's desk. He'd removed the one comfortable attorney's chair, leaving only a stiff-backed shaker for Burr when he arrived. Burr, dressed in an elegant evening suit, could well have been going to the opera. He'd sat in that rigid chair with his legs crossed and smoked with one hand while letting the ashes drop into the palm of the other.

"You had an operative in the Mills Building when my client arrived," he said.

"Yes," said Knox.

"And unless he was having coffee at the Modern Café or shopping at that pedestrian department store, he was on duty."

Knox did not proffer an answer.

"We both know what profligates that building has started to attract since it became apparent there was going to be an insurrection. As I have indicated, my client possesses information you might find acutely relevant to an ongoing or future investigation."

"We'll have him deposed and if his information proves to be reliable and valuable, then—"

"I have no intention of allowing my client to rely on the future goodwill of the federal government."

"I see. That being the case, in what small way can you be of service to us?"

"My client has unique access to certain parties operating in strict violation of American law. My client has a singular curriculum vitae that allows him to come and go freely and without exception amongst the very element that you need to unearth, investigate and ultimately indict. In short . . . for my client's services, you guarantee in writing an earned immunity."

Burr stood. He walked to the window, opened it, then flicked his ashes out into the night. He let time pass before coming about. He was smiling when he did. "It seems one of the judge's chairs is missing."

"Really?" said Knox. "I wouldn't know."

"It was here last week when I came to see him. No matter." He remained at the window, leaning back against the sill.

"One day, Mr. Knox, the government will come to the purely utilitarian decision that to efficiently and successfully deal with profligates it must enlist the services of efficient and successful profligates. As a matter of fact, I could foresee a time when our law enforcement hierarchy, the backbone of your prized bureaucracy, will all be onetime members of that wayward class."

"I guess that means my job would be in jeopardy under your definition of government service."

"Is it better to hire good men and fail, or solicit men who are . . . contra bonos mores . . . and succeed?"

Knox leaned forward. Thoughts were forming, possible plans of action, the weighing of realities. He rested his elbows on the table, set his chin on clasped and upturned hands. He studied Burr. The electric light from the wall sconce left the lawyer's complexion all the more sallow; his neck was noticeably too thin for the ruffled shirt collar. "Was it the drugs?" he asked.

Burr exhaled a rail-thin line of smoke.

"The morphine. It is morphine, that—"

"Turned me into a dissolute." Burr fingered his cigarette out the window. "I have had a taste for the unsavory . . . ever since childhood. Perhaps that's what makes me such an effective and successful attorney."

"What you are proposing would demand crossing the border, would it not?"

"Yes."

"We have no authority there."

"That doesn't mean you couldn't, or shouldn't, send an operative with him, for the gathering of evidence, the ascertainment of fact, against individuals or groups that have the potential to negatively affect domestic security. This operative could have authority over my client. We would agree to that."

"How does one have authority over someone with his biography?"

"There's a way."

"You said a few minutes ago you would never allow your client—"

"To rely on the future goodwill of the government. I emphasized the word—future."

When John Lourdes heard Justice Knox say "earned immunity" he wanted to vomit with rage. He stood in the light of that great dome trying to grasp the implications of the meeting with Burr.

"Now," said Justice Knox, "there will be an operative with him when he goes into Mexico. That operative will have complete authority, or at least tactical control. I'm considering you for this assignment."

"Sir?"

"You don't have the most field experience, but you're the only one who's truly bilingual. I'm going to be honest. I have reservations."

He kept hearing himself say, "Sir?"

"It's about character."

"Character . . . my character?"

He could feel the anger coming through in his voice.

"Not a lack of character. It's . . . I noted your reaction to Howell when we were interrogating the girl. I heard the anger in your voice just a minute ago when I told you what is going to happen. I do not question your dedication. But I need to be assured the operative I send can remain dispassionate and view this as . . . a practical application of strategy. Just as I have to remain dispassionate in my judgments."

Dispassion had been an essential condition to John Lourdes's successes. And rulership of the self demanded extreme concentration and commitment, so in certain respects Justice Knox was correct. He had failed.

"Once in Mexico, sir, I would have no legal authority over him."

"No."

"How do we control him?"

"He knows if he fails to live up to his responsibility by trying to desert, abandon or escape, your orders are to kill him. He knows if he should pose a threat to you, your orders are to kill him. He knows if anything happens to you, even if it's no fault of his, it will be the same as if he failed his responsibility. He must get you back here alive."

"Why should he follow through with any of this, if an opportunity arises?"

"Because we have something he wants."

"And that is?"

"The ability to erase his past . . . earned immunity."

There was a selfish purity to that he could understand and believe of his father, just as he could feel it in himself.

"You mean he has his own 'practical application of strategy.'"

Justice Knox's forehead furrowed deeply.

"Correct . . . now, what about my concerns with regard to you?"

"Sir, I will go wherever the practical application of strategy demands I go."

A DUFFEL AND weapons lay ready on the bed. John Lourdes sat at the desk in his room. When he'd finished his last will and testament he folded the paper neatly and edged it with a thumb, then inserted it into an envelope along with his bank book. He sealed the envelope and wrote on it: *To be opened in the event of my disappearance or death.*

The truck was parked in an empty lot behind Burr's house. Justice Knox was to bring Rawbone there clandestinely. John Lourdes arrived early as he wanted to meet with Burr alone.

Burr sat at his desk. It was littered with open law books and long-forgotten cups of coffee. The needle, as well, lay on a silk handkerchief. He wore the same ruffled shirt as the night before, and the air was spiked with marijuana smoke when Lourdes was ushered in by the silent female servant.

Burr's face took on an anguished look as he watched the young man rest his shotgun and rifle against his duffel.

"They're not here yet, as you are aware."

As John Lourdes approached the desk he removed an envelope from his coat pocket. Burr took to staring out the bay window. Across the river the red cut mountains stood out against the windless blue. He set the envelope down in front of Burr.

"What is this?"

"I'd like to hire you as my attorney."

Burr took the envelope and then turned it over. He saw what was written there.

"If I was your attorney I would advise against this quixotic nightmare."

"Are you my attorney?"

Burr nodded with despair; he would take on that duty.

A car pulled into the driveway. Knox and Howell and the murderer, turned recruit. They watched Howell walk with him to the guest quarters above the garage. Rawbone was still dressed in his suit and derby.

"He looks like a gent being escorted home after a neat bout of night prowling," said Burr.

"There's a bank book in the envelope." John Lourdes went to get his duffel and weapons. "I've signed over power of attorney. Take money for your fee. The rest is for my burial beside my mother."

Burr put the envelope down. His gaunt face looked across the room and back into a silent collection of years. "I remember how you used to sit in that chair."

John Lourdes's body arched. "So you know who I am?"

"Yes . . . I have my own detectives when I need them. I remember slipping you money one night and telling you your birth was—"

"A crime of chance."

"I saw the look on your face and regretted having said it."

"If that's an apology, I accept."

"He should never have come back. I warned him."

"Some men just can't help themselves."

"I hope you're not one of those men, John."

EIGHT

RAWBONE WAS BY the truck, giving it a close looking-over, when John Lourdes came out of the house. He still had on that derby, but now he wore a white Mexican shirt and canvas pants tucked into some hard-traveled boots. He had a bindle slung over his shoulder and his hands were pressed flat into a native sash around his waist. Knox and Howell flanked him and when he saw John Lourdes approach he tipped his hat and said, grinning, "Doctor . . . something or other . . . I presume."

John Lourdes walked right past and began to stow his belongings in the truck cab.

"What was his name?" said Rawbone to no one in particular. "I remember reading about it years ago in *The Herald*. This gent travels all of darkest Africa looking for some famous doctor and when he finds

45

him he's living in some shantytown with a tribe of spades and he says, 'Doctor so and so, I presume.' What the hell was his name?"

John Lourdes walked past him again. He joined Knox and Howell, who stood off a few yards, and they finalized plans. While he was alone Rawbone leaned around and tried to inconspicuously look down into the back of the cab housing to see if a weapon he'd nested away was still there.

The men finished their talk and shook hands. Rawbone eased away from the cab as John Lourdes approached him and said, "Get in the truck. I'll drive."

"Aye, sir," said Rawbone.

The truck rumbled out of the weeded lot, then down the driveway and past the veranda where Burr now stood watching. He had a gray stare for both men, and implicit at the heart of it was how flaws in the world so shaped human destiny.

Rawbone leaned out the cab window and called to his friend, "When I've done my penance I'll come back and then you and I can gent up and get some sinning under our belt."

He sat back and told John Lourdes, "If you ever need a righteous good attorney, he's your man. That son-of-a-bitch could have gotten Christ off."

"I can imagine," said John Lourdes, "as he seems to have done alright for Satan."

THEY DROVE IN silence through the city, then turned onto a road that led past Fort Bliss. Their destination, according to Rawbone, was somewhere in the Hueco Mountains where the arms were hidden away.

The truck scaled a rutted series of low and gravel-faced escarpments from which they could look back and see El Paso. The Rio Grande Valley had become a vast keep of civilization, with the thread of roadways and train tracks etching out in all directions and on into an ocean of heat. The valley, at that hour, on that day, so perfectly marked the years of Rawbone's wandering that he quietly cursed himself.

John Lourdes noted the vexed look on the father's face but checked it off as pure self-regard.

Rawbone turned away from the sight of El Paso. "Your name is Lourdes, right? John Lourdes?"

He eyed the father warily. "That's right."

"How do you like to be called?"

"It doesn't matter."

"It'll be Mr. Lourdes then." Rawbone reached into his pocket for a pack of cigarettes. "As befitting our stations."

John Lourdes kept to the road. But he was thinking now, I'd forgotten the voice, the tones and inflections. He had the huckster's gift to make you feel, even as he was unfaithful to anything he said.

Rawbone looked the young man over as he lit a cigarette. The khaki pants and polished boots. The vest and cravenetted Mallory hat. He was strictly Montgomery Ward's. An escapee from that blue-collar catalogue. Except for the automatic he carried in a shoulder holster.

"Is that a Browning?"

"It's a Browning."

"Cigarette?"

"I have my own."

"You from El Paso?"

"I am."

"Lourdes sounds French. Is it a French name? Are you French?"

John Lourdes leaned into the steering wheel. "It's a French name."

"You have some Mexican blood in you. I heard that."

"I am part Mexican."

"How about Anglo blood? Or is being French now considered being Anglo?"

"I have Anglo blood in me."

"You're a mutt then."

"Why not."

Rawbone set his legs up on the door frame to stretch them out. He crossed his arms. "Of course, we're all mutts, aren't we? Except for the damn Hun, who considers himself pure as some nun's noble parts." He used his cigarette as a pointer now, jabbing at the air. "Even Christ, he was a mutt. The ultimate mutt. Part man, part god. If you believe in such nonsense. What do you say to that?"

"I'm fuckin' overwhelmed."

Rawbone laughed right over that dark-eyed malicious stare and told the whole empty world around them in a booming voice, "Hey, we got a young man here who can bite without hardly opening his mouth."

HE HAS NO inkling, thought John Lourdes, not even a breath of remembrance that the one beside him in the truck is his son. John Lourdes was just another nondescript face in a tide of faces. This should have been his passport to emotional indifference, but it was not. He wanted the hard features and steady gaze to be recognized for what they were.

Soon ahead upon the plain was Fort Bliss. First they could make out the three- and two-story barracks and then row upon row of newly pitched tents. The camp had increased dramatically over the last months and there were columns of mounted infantry and supply wagons making slow headway through a steady pall of dust.

"They're getting ready for the revolution to come."

"Is that what you think?" said Rawbone. "How old are you?"

John Lourdes stared, but did not answer.

"Take a look over there. See all that artillery."

Spread out over acres of sand and sage was an armada of caissons and heavy guns.

"The Mexican is just target practice. An inconsequential. These boys are down here to drill for the war to come in Europe against the Hun and his dago bitch. The agents of war need something to practice on. Who better than some filthy, ignorant peon."

Columns of cavalry approached. John Lourdes veered toward the shoulder of the road. Rawbone swung out of the open truck and stood on the cab seat, holding to the frame with his head above the canvas roofing. As they drove along he pulled off his derby and amidst all that throated dust began to sing to the passing troops:

I'm a Yankee Doodle Dandy
A Yankee doodle do or die
A real-life nephew of my Uncle Sam
Born on the Fourth of July

That road-tired legion of riders either laughed or hurrahed and others just stared at Rawbone as if he were some sidewalk pathetic to be avoided. Yelling out, "The country is proud of you!" he swung back down into the cab.

He greeted John Lourdes's stare with a burnt wink. "Take a look at those boys, Mr. Lourdes. A good healthy look, 'cause what you're seeing there is as dumb a bunch of mules as could ever be assembled. And you know what else? They're about as equipped for where they're going as you coming with me."

NINE

J OHN LOURDES SAID nothing. He remained fixed on the task at hand. As a boy he had seen this pattern of subversion in the man. The pure willingness to destroy, even when it was contrary to his own best interests. If that's what the father now had in mind for the man named John Lourdes, then the son would meet the assault with defiant silence. Draw from that well all you want, but it isn't me, thought John Lourdes, who'll drink the water.

"That's right," said Rawbone, "pay no attention. I tend to speak on what I see. That's what comes from being a lifer at this game. Not that I have anything against those soldiers. In fact, I have a particular fondness for our military."

He took off his derby and wiped at the sweat on the inside crown with a bandana. John Lourdes looked at him, and he in turn stared back at the young man with reasoned disquiet.

"Mr. Lourdes, do you believe love can be as much a poison as hatred?"

"Very well."

"It's a wisdom alright. I was born in a place called Scabtown. A filthy pile of sewage and humankind it was. It sat across the river from Fort McKavett. San Saba County. Mostly it was built by Germans. A lot of Germans there. My mother was German. She made her living on her back. The pimp who ran the brothel used to say his girls spent so much time with their legs in the air he was surprised no one had ever tried to hoist the flag on one of them."

John Lourdes watched as the father moved through one room after another of his past. It was part of a shadow world the son had never heard, never known.

"My father, it turns out, could have been a soldier. There sure was a parade of them. Enlisted men and officers alike. Of course, he could have been some creeping Jesus of a clerk with fishbones for a spine. Or maybe some padre who had to bless his pecker every time he got hold of it. A crime of chance . . . that's what Lawyer Burr calls that kind of being born . . . a crime of chance."

Rawbone was overcome suddenly with a grimness. The unrealizable conjoined with the contradictory. Only imagine what is forward, as you cannot reimagine that which has been left behind. He was alone now in a scorching daylight with the secret company of his soul. Bitterness as raw as road dust upon the eyes.

He looked at the young man who was his warden and the young man looked away and reached for a pack of smokes in his shirt pocket. Rawbone saw and leaned over and was ready with a struck match. John Lourdes lit up from it begrudgingly. "By the way, I don't speak just to wander. I'm calling a turn here."

"Get on with it, then."

"Within two days we'll be in Juárez and I'll do my penance and be out. But you have the look of Montgomery Ward's to me and I'm not sure Montgomery Ward's will see us through."

The son stared at the father from under the brim of his hat. The face was shaded away and so the father waited.

"Do you know why you're here?" asked John Lourdes.

"Why I'm here?"

"Yes."

"Is this about my derelict life or—"

"It is not."

"Well then, why don't you tell me."

"Think about it."

"Just give me the sermon."

"You're here because of me. I brought you down."

The father sat back.

"Understand." The son's eyes flared. "You were a free man till I arrived. So I haven't done too bad so far."

East of Fort Bliss were natural springs where a stopover of sorts had been hammered up out of castoff lumber and tarpaper. There was a roadhouse the troops frequented when they were in need of a little damnation with its two eateries and a handful of merchandisers and a part-time brothel in a mechanics' shed. It always had its share of travelers, this being the main thoroughfare between El Paso and Carlsbad.

It was here they pulled off the road. And while John Lourdes checked the radiator and filled the gas tank from one of a set of drums lashed down in the truckbed, Rawbone hit the roadhouse to stack up on a few beers for the drive to the Huecos, where he'd hidden away the armaments.

John Lourdes leaned against the truckbed and looked toward the mountains. He was considering how best to preserve himself while carrying an illegal cargo of contraband into Mexican territory.

"I'm Goddamn envious."

He turned. Approaching was a man with a broad face and stiff mustache. He had a ruddy smile and a laborer's body, but his clothes spoke of someone well appointed.

"Fine truck. One of those new three-tonners, isn't it?"

"Yes, sir."

The man was bowlegged and hitched some when he walked. "Mind if I look her over?"

"No, sir."

He walked the chassis, admiring the workmanship with an unerring eye and a taste for detail. He pointed to AMERICAN PARTHENON painted on the siding. "That your company?"

"No sir. I'm just a driver."

"Well, you look like a climber to me." He winked. Then he looked over the cab interior, studying the steering wheel and shift, the floor starter. "Keep an eye to the future, son. It's exciting times. God, what I would give to be your age now."

Rawbone walked up to the truck. He was carrying a couple of bottles of beer and he put them on the cab seat. He'd overheard the man, who now looked at him. "Your partner there can tell you. It all goes by quick as a piss. Look to the future, son, like you were at those mountains a few minutes ago. Damn, what I wouldn't give to take the ride again—"

As the man walked away, John Lourdes came around the truck. Rawbone said, "I hope me buying you a beer doesn't constitute a bribe."

"Get in the truck. We're rolling out of here now. You drive."

The truck rumbled out into the roadway and made for the east. John Lourdes crabbed through his duffel till he found binoculars.

"What's got you, Mr. Lourdes?"

"He was admiring the truck alright, but it was my shoulder holster and the weapons in the cab that clocked most of his interest."

The father glanced back toward the springs as the son focused his binoculars. Through the dazzling heat a tight pack of men on horseback and one on a motorcycle made the road and started their way. The motorcycle sped out and took the lead.

"At least four riders, one motorcycle."

"Was he one of them?"

"Too much dust."

"They could be road thugs."

"Or worse."

"Is there a weapon anywhere in my future, Mr. Lourdes?"

"I'm no fortuneteller."

"Well, I guess I'll have a beer then."

THE MOTORCYCLE WAS far in advance of the horsemen but not so far back it could not keep the truck in sight. A stand would have to be made. That was becoming more obvious with the failing light. John Lourdes decided it should be the place where the weapons had been cached away. They ascended the windswept remains of a cart path into the Huecos. The rocks hulked up in the paling light on all sides to become brooding silhouettes. The silence deepened till there was only the sound of that laboring engine.

On a plat of ground surrounded by shaly hills were the crumbling walls of a village. A single block of adobes led to a roofless meeting hall of two stories. The wind had begun to rise up and that barren range became engulfed in a deepening sense of isolation and emptiness. The sun on a far promontory burned with the last of the day. John Lourdes traced that cart path down through the hills as best he could with his binoculars for any sign of their pursuers.

"It'll be two hours yet," said Rawbone, "before those horsemen catch up with the one on the motorcycle. And that long again to sneak their way up here."

"Where are the weapons?"

"Why, Mr. Lourdes, they're in plain sight."

And they were, in a manner of speaking. The father had the son follow him beyond the meeting house to a sandy incline scarred with crevasses. Then he waved the son to keep step behind as he scaled that crag following a plumb line of fist-sized stones and upon reaching the last near the apex, squatted down.

"Notice the line of rocks. They mark the spot. Now. Stand close, Mr. Lourdes, and watch the magic."

The father reached into the sand and his arms vanished near up to the elbows. As he pulled the sand began to ribbon and twill and the hill face moved like the back of some hidden monster coming to life.

"Kneel down here and light a match."

A vein of light fell upon the stacked crates hidden there in a recess beneath a tarp that had been covered by sand.

"What all is down there?"

"Your garden-variety arsenal. Carbines, ammunition, hand grenades, dynamite and detonators, and a .50 caliber machine gun. Mr. Lourdes, you could hold off the Holy Roman Empire with all that firepower."

John Lourdes blew out the match.

JOHN LOURDES HAD Rawbone move the truck far back of the meeting house and away from where the weapons were cached. He swung the shotgun strap over his shoulder. He carried rifle and binoculars loose. While he ran to a place from where he would watch the road Rawbone, alone now, slipped down under the chassis.

Before arriving in El Paso, Rawbone had hammered a strip of flap leather to the underside of the chassis housing. He'd nailed it into the wood on three sides, leaving the fourth open to form a sort of pocket or pouch where he stashed away an automatic. When that was done he'd hammered the last side closed so the weapon wouldn't shake loose.

TEN

THE SKYLINE WAS settling out, the blue softening away till there was only the marked approach of nightfall. John Lourdes sat in silence near the headway of the plat. Rawbone approached and stood near, scanning the moonless world to the road below.

"You have any idea how you intend to make this fight?"

John Lourdes was staring up that street of crumbling foundations to the meeting house. "What was this place? Do you know?"

Rawbone ran the back of his fingers along his cheek. "You never heard and you're from El Paso?" He set the derby back. "It was one of those . . . utopias. You know what they are, right? Well . . . this one was different. There was only women. Women from all over the world. Anglo women, Mexican. Women from India. China. Even Africa. They lived like a tribe. And they had ceremonies where they went about na-ked. Naked, Mr. Lourdes."

The son now looked upon those forgotten remains and tried to imagine—

The father threw his head back laughing. "Mr. Lourdes, if ever I saw an expression of pure and ridiculous gullibility." He shook his head in comedic despair.

The son was forced to accept the moment and he took it stoically, but not without a smile that he was had. "By the way," John Lourdes asked, "did you retrieve the gun?"

Rawbone cocked his head. "Excuse me?"

"The automatic stashed under the chassis. I checked the damn vehicle early this morning."

Rawbone pulled up his shirt where the gun had been tucked away. "Mr. Lourdes, the tide of opinion about you has just risen some." He pulled the weapon and held the black .32 just so in his palm and, mocking, added, "Bat Masterson swears by this gun. Or so says the ad. And another promises . . . it's a housewife's best friend against burglars." He tucked the shirt back in his pants and slipped the weapon down into his belt sash. He paused to set his derby right. "Mr. Lourdes, it's a right-thinking world when they start running ads with guns and women in nightgowns."

The son went back to considering how a fight was to be made. The father stood watch. And so the night went about its workings.

"Mr. Lourdes, do you come from a good Christian family?"

The son looked up at the father and in a pointed quiet said, "In part."

"Well, you better pack that good Christian part away for a while . . . because they're here."

John Lourdes rose. He looked down into that banded decline of shadows but saw nothing. Rawbone stepped behind him and pointed, his arm resting just over the rim of the son's shoulders. There was a narrow slit of brightness, not even really a light, for one moment. "Far, far down the canyon. There! Did you see it?"

"No."

"I believe it's one of those flashlights with the sliding bridge slip. You know. And they're keeping it near to the ground so all you see is a bit of wash from the light."

The father was so close now the son could feel the weapon he had tucked away pressing against his back.

"You can't look right at a thing at night that far to see it, Mr. Lourdes. The trick is you have to look off just a bit. Use the outer ring of your eye."

The son did as the father said and in the space of a minute there was a singular emanation so minute as to be barely made out.

"Yes," said John Lourdes, "I see it. You're right."

"That's a trick you learn from years of being on the hunt."

The son turned. "You mean being hunted, don't you?"

"That too, Mr. Lourdes. But when they're as close as you and I are now, hunter and hunted, it's all the same."

John Lourdes studied the man he was born of. "Is that a threat, or a word of advice?"

"I leave it to your good judgment, sir. But either way, the clock is about to expire on the quiet around here."

THE PLAT WHERE the settlement had been was akin to a darkened lake that night. Father and son crouched on elbows. Men appeared in slow and hunched silence from the foothills. The father rose three fingers and the son agreed.

They approached low behind their guns, totally unaware their souls might well be swallowed up. A wind sprang from nowhere and sent dust across the broken terrain. The father whispered to the son, "How well do you hear?"

"Why?"

The father touched his ear and held up one finger and pointed toward the rocks beyond the meeting house. The son understood.

"I'll give that one a hello for you." Then Rawbone snaked up the ravine from where they lay in wait till there was only the faint movement of loose shale where he had just been.

John Lourdes now stayed rigid against the earth. He had never killed before and this would be something else altogether. Those figures of the night reached the adobe foundations. They must not be thought of as men. They are just vestments really. Blackish shapes there to extinguish life. They started their slow and deadly trek up that once-upon-a-time street. The night had not grown colder, yet John Lourdes was shivering. The wind moved through his clothes like the ghost of something insidious and horrible.

These men will kill without so much as a reckoning. They will fire down till you're not even one whittled breath. One of the men put out a hand for the others to stop. He took a few cautious steps forward and John Lourdes recognized the bowed and partly lame stride as belonging to the gent at the roadhouse with the stiff mustache and cheery smile. He had seen something. John Lourdes hoped it was the bedrolls laid out like sleeping men within the meeting house walls.

They moved ahead again with the steady assurance of those who had imperiled men before. He watched their stalk play out like a ritual. There was a stark grace to their configured tactics, a calm John Lourdes did not possess.

The meeting house stood against the night sky. Its hollowed windows and huge gaping frame that once housed double doors the epitome of emptiness.

John Lourdes scanned that rutted wash where Rawbone had gone. He listened with dire intensity, but there was only the wind through dry brush like flintstrikings. A vein in his temple pulsed vengefully.

When they reached the meeting house door the men fanned out. They pressed in close to the adobe wall and near blended away. The one from the roadhouse raised a hand to make ready and as he did John

Lourdes also reached out his hand where it hovered in dead space just above a detonator. He could feel the hand trembling all the way up into the sinew of his neck.

Even though John Lourdes was waiting and ready, their charge into the hollows happened so fast he froze. The walls flashed with the thunder light of their weapons. Arterials of smoke and powdered cloth leapt from the bedrolls. But there was not a cry, not a breath of movement that declared life was being taken.

The bedrolls lay there like the lifeless bait they were. The men understood immediately and scattered. It was only then, at the last, before all advantage had been lost, that John Lourdes found himself. With the flat of his hand he drove down the plunger.

ELEVEN

JOHN LOURDES HAD set the charge by the meeting house wall, burrowing dynamite into the sand, while Rawbone used a clump of sage to brush away any signs of that long run of wire to the detonator.

There was a momentary harnessing of raw power. The front of the building was torn asunder and disappeared in an avalanche of smoke. The concussion echoed far out into the hills. The men were flung like paltry cloth dolls and from the sky a storm of adobe and rock hailed across that plat.

John Lourdes rose now with his rifle ready and started into that smoky destruction, when far to his right there came the rapid action of an automatic. He came about and knelt, the rifle anchored up on his shoulder. Through the settling dust came a man running. He held his back and was calling in desperation to his friends. He stumbled and his boots dragged up a rising trail of dust. He collapsed to his knees and that is where Rawbone ran him down. He came out of the dark leaping from the rocks and put two more shots into the sagging body, which lurched forward at the last.

He sprinted past the son, yelling, "Make sure they're all dead!" He kept on through the haze. "I'll take it to the road and introduce myself to any fool they might have left with the horses."

John Lourdes walked the destruction. It was otherworldly. He could not fathom truly being there. The smell of charred clothes and flesh tainted the air and he worried it might poison him in some unknown way. He came upon the first, who lay on his side. There was nothing below the upper lip but a bloody shirt collar. Then he noted what he thought to be an odd necklace dangling down the man's face before he realized it was an eye loosed of its socket and hanging by a long thread of muscle.

The next man lay on his stomach. John Lourdes knelt and eased the body over. The dark and lifeless face he came to see belonged to the man who'd faced him down in Juárez, the father of the girl Teresa. He stood. He stared down at this stranger on the other side of death. Questions abounded.

Pilings of wood on the meeting house floor had caught fire. The air was singed with windblown ash. John Lourdes had to cover his face as he turned toward the last man, the one from the roadhouse.

He sat against a backdrop of adobe and rotted timber beams. He was not dead, though he should have been as the shape of his head was hideously altered.

From up the cart path came a headway of trampling hooves. Riderless mounts plunged headlong from the shadows hounded by gunshots and the gritty musculature of a motorcycle engine. Rawbone had herded up the horses. He yelled out as he wheeled in the motorcycle, "There was a last one down by the main road."

Cinders from the fire were now a burning rain everywhere and Rawbone took to using his derby to swipe them from his eyes as he joined up with John Lourdes. "We better board up and be on with it. If any of these sparks find their way to—"

The man from the roadhouse sat staring up at them. The father squatted. The man was gibbering away, yet there looked to be in his eyes a degree of consciousness and understanding. In his hand was the flashlight. Rawbone slipped it loose. He switched on the light and put it to the man's face. It mooned out of the dark. Blood seeped from a crack in the skull along the forehead. A bit of brain matter protruded from the wound, looking like the marbled head of a snail.

"He's leaking oil, Mr. Lourdes."

Rawbone stood.

"It's your watch, Mr. Lourdes."

The son understood. It was either finish him or forget him, as he was for the wolves. The father waited. He held his derby against the onslaught of scorched ash and heat.

"The fire, Mr. Lourdes. One spark could send us off."

He saw something pass over John Lourdes's face. A brief moment of the soul perhaps, of what had to be. It was not a look of indecision, but rather something more reflective of true human reluctance, or even a tragic pity. It mattered none. Rawbone had no place for either and hated each equally. He reached for his belted automatic, but John Lourdes grabbed his wrist and restrained him. Now, the father prided himself on strong arms, all the more so for a man his size, and he felt in the son's grip the same pure hard strength.

"Strip each body of everything in their pockets," said John Lourdes. "Wallets, any scrap of paper. Leave nothing. Collect it for me. Saddlebags too."

"Mr. Lourdes . . ."

The son ordered him again in no uncertain terms and the father walked off. "Why don't I do that, Mr. Lourdes. That'll give you some time to negotiate the matter at hand with your conscience."

A moment later there was a gunshot that caused the horses to startle and scatter. The father turned. The impact had driven the man to the earth, where charred cinders blew over him. With a streak of pure mean Rawbone mocked what the dead man had said down at the roadhouse. "The way I see you by that truck, looking off to the hills . . . you're a real climber, son."

TWELVE

A FEW LAST SCATTERED sparks blew from that barren upland as the truck descended to the road. They had it rigged up and strapped down with the trappings of war. They'd even lashed the motorcycle, like some trophy from a battle of yore, to the truckbed.

It was a matter now of the crossing into Mexico. The main bridges over the Rio Grande with their immigration agents and customs officers posed too much of a threat and so were out of the question. And finding shallows you would gamble a truck might navigate would be a marvel of stupidity. But Rawbone knew of a rope ferry south of El Paso near the old Socorro Mission. The river had changed course there near a half-century before, and was a place of isolated sandbars and lonely stretches of shoreline.

They drove through the chilly hours before dawn. A smoky oil lamp hung from the roof frame above the son's head. The father's upturned derby rested on the cab seat between both men. It was filled to the brim with what Rawbone had scavenged from the dead as John Lourdes had ordered. Rawbone watched as John Lourdes meticulously studied each personal item, every bit of identification, holding them up to the trundling light, eyes squinting from the grainy smoke to better read ink that had faded with wear. He would then write certain details down in a pocket notebook he carried. His concentration stayed exact and his hand steady even as the truck pitched and rose on that worthless road.

It seemed to Rawbone he himself did not even exist during these hours. He was, in fact, left to his own private maelstroms and outside the fitted plan. This fed a sense of disadvantage and that always left him uncertain and wary. "Why all the looking and writing, Mr. Lourdes?"

He glanced up from his notebook. "I noticed," he said, "there's no paper money in that derby of yours."

"You didn't order me to grub the dead for your salary."

"I suppose you left it to the buzzards as a charitable donation."

"As a matter of fact, my notion was to buy you something when we're done. In memorial of our time together."

John Lourdes went back to his notebook.

"You didn't answer me, Mr. Lourdes."

"I didn't answer."

"That much I know."

John Lourdes looked up again. He slipped the pencil behind his ear, set the notebook in his lap. He began with the girl at the fumigation building, then following her into Mexico and sketching in a series of strange incidents that took him to that morning at the Mills Building.

Rawbone leaned back and scratched at his cheek with the edge of a thumb. "If I ever meet her, I'll have to remember to thank her for the introduction."

"One of the dead back on that mountain. The Mexican. That was her father."

That detail was like a stone dropped into a pond of still water and the ripples it sent through Rawbone's mind. He said, "I see now."

"Do you?"

"If you want to get to the heart of something, cut away."

John Lourdes had been thinking out how the dead back up on that mountain came to know about him and the truck. It seemed apparent. Mr. Simic and his associates had come upon an alternate way to resolve their unfortunate problem—they notified the people they were supplying that the truck and its cache of munitions had been taken. Rawbone leaned into the steering wheel and listened with unsettling intensity. They had to know the truck had been taken somewhere between Carlsbad and El Paso, so it was likely the munitions were hidden away somewhere not so easily discovered. With only one road between the two cities, how difficult would it be to watch for a truck painted up with lettering like the top of a birthday cake, well—

He was staring toward the dark mesas that stood between him and his immunity when John Lourdes said, "There's something else that you . . . we . . . need to consider."

"Have at it, Mr. Lourdes."

"Any advantage you . . . we . . . had is gone. When some of theirs don't return and you come driving up with that truck—"

"It will sure make for conversation, won't it?"

"You know where we're going in Juárez and who we're to talk to. That was part of the deal. Alright. But my responsibility is to discover the names and/or identities of anyone and everyone involved or connected to this criminal enterprise. That's why I had you grab up all those men's personals." He held up the notebook. "That's what I'm writing here. That's why I'm telling you all this now. Those dead back up there in the mountains will have some say on what is going to happen when we reach Juárez."

When John Lourdes had his say, he went back to his work without so much as another word, leaving Rawbone with a reality for which there was no apparent solution. He took a cigarette from its pack. He struck a match on the steering column. His mind was being drawn into the unseen ahead, and the survivor in him began to coolly plot what would best serve him.

"Are you a schooled man, Mr. Lourdes?"

John Lourdes finished what he was noting and then looked up. The question went to the flashpoint of his life. "Oil boy in the roundhouses at thirteen. Railroad detective for the Santa Fe at twenty. Then the BOI. A few night classes in between."

"All that with only a notepad and some native instinct."

"You're never at a loss, are you?"

"I've misfired a time or two."

"But you're always right there and ready to help someone drown."

"With a smile and good cheer."

"We'll have this done in another day, so let's not stumble-fuck over each other. Then you can get on with your miserable existence as a free man."

"I couldn't have said it better myself."

John Lourdes returned to his notebook. He took up the last wallet from the derby.

"I think you misunderstood me," said Rawbone.

"Did I?"

"I only meant you've a clear mind, and it's carried you well."

Even before the sun, came the heat. It was going to be that kind of day. The shadows fell away behind them as the sun rose over the rim of the world and bore light down upon their road.

The last wallet belonged to the man who'd spoken to John Lourdes at the roadhouse. His name was James Merrill. In a side pouch was a tiny print of him in uniform standing before a harbored warship with other members of his squad.

"The one from the roadhouse," said John Lourdes, "must have served in Cuba during the Spanish-American War."

Rawbone leaned back to try and get a look. He asked for the photo. He held it against the steering wheel. The dun-colored print was badly beaten at the edges and deeply faded. It was a moment caught bare. Soldiers laughing and at the ready. Serve a cause, change the world. It was not worth spit now. That's what death had to say about it all. There is only the ever selfish present to consider. Yet even so—

He handed back the photo. "That warship is the China," said the father, "and that's not Cuba, but Manila harbor."

His gaze returned to the road. It was an impossible leap for the son to imagine the father anywhere people embark upon a cause. Yet how else could he have known so quickly?

He went back to the wallet. In another pocket he found a cache of business cards all neatly printed and fairly new. What was written there was sobering to a fault.

They were driving in a region where the earth had been thrust up through the faults of time and the ragged line of rocks the road divided looked as if they had been shaped by a hostile blade saw. The son turned the business cards over and over in his hand.

"There's something here that falls short."

Rawbone glanced at John Lourdes, who handed him the business card. The father held it up and read:

JAMES MERRILL
STANDARD OIL COMPANY
MEXICO

THIRTEEN

THE SOCORRO MISSION was on the El Camino de Tierra Adentro just southeast of the ford where the ferry crossed the Rio Grande. Constructed on a sandy incline, the church was a simple structure with a stepped parapet above the front door on which sat the bell tower.

It was late afternoon when the truck labored up to the low mud brick wall that flanked the nave and from where they could view the ferry. The church was quiet. A few gulls sat atop the bell tower with its cross. There was no shade save for one manzanita alongside the adobe wall. The men rested there in the stifling heat and studied the ferry.

It was docked on the Texas side. There was a customs shack on each shoreline. On this side of the river, the shack stood within a small grotto of trees. The one on the opposing shore stood bare in a landscape that looked like the unfinished country of God's hand. It was still as a painting down there.

"Keep the truck company," said Rawbone. "I'll go to the river to get the feel of things. See what all we have to deal with."

John Lourdes walked to the truck and removed his shoulder holster and set it on the cab seat. He couldn't help but keep looking at the mission. From the moment they'd driven up to this lonely spot he felt as if voices from the other world were talking to him.

There was a pump down one side of the building with a boiler that had been blowtorched in half then plunked down in the sand to use as a trough. He removed his vest and shirt to shave. It was then he remembered the crucifix around his neck, the one with the broken cross beam that was his mother's. Realizing it might give him away, he slipped it off and hid it in his wallet.

JOHN LOURDES WENT into the cool and quiet of the church to wait. Something about this mission held him. Inside it was as simple as the faith that inspired it. It was the faith of his mother and her people, the faith that spoke of sacrifice, of mercy and forgiveness.

There was a statue of the crucified Christ near tall as he was beside the pulpit. There was also a pedestal that stood before the side pews holding a statue of the Virgin and Child. That is where he sat. He placed his hat beside him. Light from the windows cast dusk upon the floor. He studied the Madonna's face, the pale skin of the European, the painted stare a conception of immaculate calm and peace. What was it about this place—

"Praying?"

Caught off guard, John Lourdes came quickly around. Rawbone had entered the mission silently. He sat in the pew across from John Lourdes. He glanced at the statue of the Virgin and Child. "If you're praying to her, forget it. She sure didn't do shit for her son." Then those dusty loveless eyes motioned toward the cross.

To that John Lourdes had nothing to say. He took his hat and stood to leave. Rawbone motioned he sit again. "Nothing can happen till dark anyway."

The son sat.

The father seemed to have something on his mind.

"When you were a detective for the Santa Fe you must have worked the yards by the river."

"I did."

"You probably met a lot of people from the barrio."

"I did."

"You being part Mexican."

"I speak the language, if that's what you mean."

"I was talking about families and such. Knowing families and such."

"Families and such . . . yes."

Rawbone sat a bit longer, taking in all that was about him.

"Why do you ask?" said John Lourdes.

Something moved those features momentarily.

"Another time."

He stood.

"We only have tomorrow," said John Lourdes.

"That's right. Let's see then how that goes. For both of us."

Had what he'd seen been the substance of unspeakable regret, or unresolved sorrow? And if it was, what of it? As Rawbone walked out John Lourdes asked, "How do you know this place?"

The father turned and with a way the son well remembered, said, "I was married here, Mr. Lourdes." With that he tapped down his derby and started to the door. "Go back to your mysteries, Mr. Lourdes. I'll be outside . . . after I rob the poorbox."

The river lay in darkness. There were but token lights down by the ferry. Music could be heard coming from the shack on the Rio Bravo side. Rawbone had his bindle open on the cab seat when John Lourdes joined him.

"How do we go about the crossing?"

Rawbone took a bottle of whiskey and a flask from the bindle. "We . . . I'm going entertaining. When it's clear to make the ferry, I'll sight you up with a lantern."

He walked away with the whiskey tucked up under his arm, whistling as if he were on a Friday night adventure.

The son watched the ferry landing from the adobe wall and smoked. Through binoculars he saw Rawbone approach the shack on the Rio Bravo side. The men, there were three, moved into the doorway light as the flatbed touched shore. Rawbone began talking, pointing with an arm, first in one direction, then the other. But always it was the arm that had the whiskey bottle. His gestures were pure story. The men measured him with their eyes, but it wasn't long before he'd hustled up an invitation into their world.

From time to time, John Lourdes glanced back at the church. Now he understood why somewhere in the fretwork of his memories this mission had its place.

A LIGHT APPEARED at the river. It began to firefly as the father flagged a lantern with his derby. On the American side a man briefly peered out a shack window as the truck geared through its shifts to the landing. The ferry swayed under the weight of the vehicle, the current slapped dangerously up against its sides. Pulling the haul rope was slow and difficult, and John Lourdes kept a ready watch, knowing at that moment he'd gone past the last vestiges of American law.

As the truck labored up from the ferry Rawbone leapt the sideboard. "So far from God, so close to the U.S.," he said. "Let's get from here."

John Lourdes fed the gas. The engine pulled and they passed slowly the pitiful tarpaper and adobe border station. The acute quiet caught John Lourdes's attention immediately.

No one in sight, the door partly open. He tried to spy in.

"No need to involve yourself, Mr. Lourdes."

There was a faint trace in the father's voice that had the feel of the awful. It wasn't until the last, as the truck veered into the road and away from the shack, he noticed back beyond the doorway in the half dark a chair knocked over. Rising up in him was a stirring uncertainty that John Lourdes, even against his better judgment, needed to address.

He pulled the truck over and jumped down from the cab. He started for the border station.

"I wouldn't," said the father.

FOURTEEN

THE ROOM WAS a scene of pitiless death. Burning candles filled that space with shadows. The bodies lay like twisted sculptures of suffering. One on the floor was doubled up, another's head arched back on a bed, the face a twisted apotheosis of horror. White froth had accumulated about the mouth. Flies already skimmed the flesh. John Lourdes stepped from the shack and the night closed in all around him. He walked to the truck where Rawbone sat behind the wheel with the motor idling.

"Shall we be on?" he asked.

"I forgot, for a moment. You're just a common assassin."

"I beg to argue, Mr. Lourdes. I am a most uncommon assassin."

John Lourdes looked back across the river.

Rawbone repeated, "So far from God, so close to the U.S."

John Lourdes closed his eyes.

"What did you think, young sir? That we would cross just as easy as buying sheets and pillows? A little liquor, a little cash? These campesinos may be street dirt and dumb as a brick, but they can sniff out a score with the truest of them."

"So you just murdered—"

"That's where you're wrong."

The son turned to the father.

"No, no, no. We murdered three men."

John Lourdes's eyes narrowed.

"We took this truck into Mexico. We are taking this truck filled with munitions to Juárez. We are together."

"I see."

"Do you, Mr. Lourdes? I'm circumspect. So just in case. Once we crossed that river and left behind everything you're built on, you became as much my field hand as I am yours. And those three," he pointed with his derby toward the shed, "seal the contract. And we'll sleep the sleep on it."

John Lourdes pushed his hat back and leaned into the cab. "Sleep the sleep, I won't forget that. No . . . I won't."

"Ready to mingle it up with me? Let me remind you of something. Of a conversation Lawyer Burr had with your Justice Knox about my coming. He had a name for it. A phrase. The practical—"

"—the practical application of strategy."

"There you go. That street dirt back there in the shack, they are the practical application of strategy."

"For your benefit."

"Absolute. It's a means of holding you to the cross. I don't think your Justice Knox would care to see one of his own standing trial in a foreign country for a murder committed because of an order the BOI issued. That doesn't seem to me . . . a practical application of strategy."

There was a grim flicker of dark accomplishment.

"How did you come to exist?" said John Lourdes.

"I came to exist in the same manner as Cain and Abel. Then I was baptized pure American for good measure."

THE LIGHTS OF Juárez stood out upon the plain. The road they were on followed the trackline. The way was lit by intermittent campfires with small groups of raggletag peons brandishing weapons. Soldiers in the making. An army of insurrection rising up out of the evening land. Their voices wild and bitter and ready to war.

"Mr. Lourdes, if they knew what we were carting . . . the bad news for you, we'd spend eternity like some married couple in a common grave."

They had been riding in silence since the river. Until that moment. John Lourdes now said, "I want to know now who you are to meet, and where."

Rawbone considered. "By tomorrow you'll be sleeping in your own bed and maybe supping at the Modern Café there in the lobby of the Mills Building."

"I want to know."

There was gunfire and the footfalls of men. John Lourdes came about quickly, his hand going to the shoulder holster. Rawbone stayed to the wheel. Men rushed past the truck to a fight that had flared there by the roadside.

The son turned his attention back to the father, who'd still not even once looked away from the road. "Who and where?"

"Is this a test of wills?"

"If something should happen to you."

"Haven't you even heard the rumor that just thinking it can bring down bad luck? You wouldn't want that."

"My job is to see this through."

"As is mine."

"But I chose to be here. Grant me the information."

Rawbone did not answer. John Lourdes was left to wait, and wait. Then, as if an afterthought, the father said, "Alliance for Progress. Just up from the Customs House on September 16 Avenue. Hecht is the man Simic told me to address."

John Lourdes wrote all this down in his notebook. As he did, from one of the campfires came a boy in near rags running with hat in hand up alongside the truck and begging for money. The father reached into his pocket and asked the son, "The man's name from the roadhouse?"

The son scanned his notes. "James Merrill."

The father tossed the boy a crumpled buck and told him in Spanish, "Courtesy of Mr. James Merrill."

The boy took the money and swung his hat in thanks.

"Before we confront this Hecht fellow," said John Lourdes, "we have to deal with protecting the truck."

"We?"

"Where you go—I go. Where I go—you go."

"With that in mind, Mr. Lourdes. I have a place you'll find particularly fitting."

THEY DROVE THROUGH a neighborhood of blistered hovels and empty lots along the shore. Laundry hung from lines in the starlight. The smell of meals cooking in greased pans scented the air. Somewhere a mother tried to calm a crying child; somewhere there was music and laughter. It was a mirror of the barrio they could see across the streaming quiet of the river, where they'd existed once upon a time with a woman one married and the other called mother. A moment fell through time. A moment they shared without knowing because of the flaw in their existence.

At the end of that long, filthy street was factory row. There the truck pulled up to a drab squat building with a rotting sign on the roof: RODRIGUEZ FUNERARIA.

84

A funeral parlor.

John Lourdes asked, "You're not trying to politely tell me something, are you?"

In the gray dark Rawbone only grinned and stepped from the cab.

The door opened into what had been an entrance hall. Heavy drapes hung from garish rodding along the walls. The oxblood cloth was moth-eaten and smelled of must. The room was empty but for a desk, where a man slept all bundled up with his hands tucked under his head as a pillow. A black cloth covered a doorway and from beyond came a dramatic overture issuing from a piano.

Rawbone dragged the sleeping man from the desk and told him in no uncertain Spanish he was a ball-less toad and he better do as he was damn well ordered and let McManus know Rawbone was here.

The man went out stoop-shouldered and mumbling. The father had the son follow him through the covered doorway. As the tarp was pulled back John Lourdes found himself at the rear of a room that had once been for the viewing of bodies but was now a theatre for the showing of movies.

People sat on poorly nailed-together benches while an old Mexican in a Florentine suit played an upright that looked as if it might have made the trip over with Columbus. There was a smoky grit to the light from the projector and on the screen came the flickering rush of images:

BRONCO BILLY ANDERSON

IN

THE ROAD AGENTS

Father and son remained back by the entranceway. The black cutouts that were people shadows watching the movie more than likely knew little or no English to understand the scene cards, but it mattered not at all. When the road agents thundered down on that stagecoach and robbed the payroll box, the outlaw emotion in the audience rose to the moment. Cheering wildly and screaming of revolution and down with Díaz and the government pistols were fired into the air. Chips of plaster and dust rained everywhere as the room stenched with powdersmoke.

The son looked to the father. Framed in grainy illumination Rawbone was intent upon the screen as the posse formed up for the hunt. His eyes flashed and his mouth opened and his lips reared back in anticipation as one bandit beat down the other over greed and rode off with the ill-gotten gains.

Rawbone leaned toward John Lourdes and spoke behind the cover of his hand: "I love the nickelodeon. Wished they had 'em when I was a boy. That's a world to be introduced to. There's only one thing they can't show right. Movies, I mean. And you know what that is?"

The son had no idea. The father held his hands together as if the fragile and the priceless rested there. "The dyin'," he said. "They can't get that right. The horror when a gent knows all trace of him is being wiped out of existence. The knowing you will be no more. For that's the only thing there is, one's own living self."

FIFTEEN

McMANUS CAME THROUGH the doorway like a wind, all hail
and hearty hellos for his friend, dragging Rawbone out into
the atrium where they embraced and cursed each other.

McManus was a great hulk of a man with a flabby nose and a
quarter-size chin. He was also missing an arm, the left one. He wore
a prosthesis up past the elbow with a shaped wooden oval wrist and
detachable wooden hand. The fingers, oddly, were spread out wide as
if in a state of perpetual surprise. And the arm itself looked to be a
few sizes too small for him, as it was at least six inches shorter than
the other. It was with this arm and hand he pointed at John Lourdes.
"What is this?"

"This . . . is a Mr. Lourdes."

"Really. One of those, heh. Did you serve in Manila, Mr. Lourdes?
Is that how you came to be under the spell of this bugger?"

"Look at him, you brainless shit. He would have been a boy."

"They had boys fighting that were thirteen."

"Mr. Lourdes, would you mind," said Rawbone, "waiting by the truck."

The tenor of the two men's talk changed immediately upon John Lourdes leaving.

"Since when did you start running a boy's home?"

"Since I was . . . engaged . . . to work with a certain former railroad detective on a . . . particular matter."

McManus jerked a thumb toward the outside. "That one?"

"That one."

"If he don't look like a lightning bug trying to pass for lightning."

"I got a truck outside that needs to be parked away in your ware-house till morning. You will be neatly compensated for your charity."

"By the lightning bug?"

JOHN LOURDES WAITED by the truck. The dead from the mountain and the river were with him in the dark, still in their assigned poses at the moment of demise. He wondered now, did God see man as this threadbare and vanquished figure infected with his own immorality? Yet, with all that on his mind and soul, the single overriding principle he clung to was—the practical application of strategy. The door opened and both men approached.

"You can be free with my friend here," said Rawbone. "I've told him you had been a railroad detective and . . . we were engaged in a particular matter. And there would be money for the use of his warehouse."

Stepping up into the cab seat, he added, "You wait here, Mr. Lourdes. I'm gonna bed down this truck."

The night had cooled and John Lourdes grabbed an old leather coat from the back. Rawbone drove off leaving him with McManus.

They stood in the doorway shadowed together and watching the truck gear slowly around the corner. John Lourdes looked at McManus. McManus smiled down at the young man, but it was not a heartening smile.

"So, you were in the war," said John Lourdes.

"Part of the Texas Battalion. Served with Rawbone. In Manila."

"I didn't know that."

"They say the best soldiers are the biggest bastards."

"That would mean he'd qualify."

This drew a genuine laugh from McManus. "Two medals, and he's not even a fuckin' patriot."

The idea that Rawbone had ever fought for the country set off a run of thoughts. "Do you know a man named Merrill? He served in Manila. Was with Standard Oil in Mexico."

"No."

John Lourdes reached into his vest pocket. When McManus saw the notepad, he commented, "I make it a habit of not remembering names."

John Lourdes understood. "You won't even be a mention."

McManus answered, "Comforting."

But John Lourdes suspected he now wasn't so sure. The photo and business cards were tucked away in the notepad. He handed the weathered print to McManus, who set it in the palm of his wooden hand. Holding it close, he squinted. "I don't know this man."

"Are you familiar with the Alliance for Progress?"

SON AND FATHER walked obscure and wretched streets past beggars in doorways and broken-down bars and past children huddled up in makeshift boxes that were all they had for homes. Rawbone eyed the urchins and knew himself in their deserted stares. As they made for the appointed destination dragoons rode past in slow, watchful columns.

The late-night patrols another sign Mexico was about to be taken by nightmare. He got out a cigarette and lit it.

John Lourdes still had the photo in his hand and kept tapping it against his shoulder holster as they went. He was making a determined inventory of the facts at hand to try and distill what he knew into a plan that would fulfill his orders.

"McManus said you were in the army."

"Yeah."

"He said you served with the Texas Battalion."

"Yeah."

"Were they posted at Fort Bliss or San Antonio?"

"Fort Bliss."

Rawbone was preoccupied. He blew the smoke out his nostrils hard. He wanted this night over, he wanted Mr. Lourdes out of his life, he wanted freedom.

"Did you spend a lot of time in El Paso during those years?"

"What is it with the questions?"

"You were asking me at the church about the barrio and did I know families there. I just wondered—"

"Yeah." The question went right to the pitiful bits of truth he did not want any part of tonight. Tonight was about survival. Fuck the agony of remembered ghosts—for now. "The army wasn't much," he said. "I needed time out of the States. The war, though. If you have the temperament for it, war can be a blessing."

"What were the medals for?"

He tossed the cigarette away. "Killing, of course."

THE VIEJA ADUANA was a block-long building with a clocktower above the main entryway. The facing was all Palladian windows and the interior lit so bright the Customs House seemed to be on fire. Son and father could see the lobby was crowded with men, so many they were spilling out into the street where frontier customs guards stood at the watch. Most of the men, be they nationals or foreigners, were of the business and mercantile class, suited and without guns. But there were also rough verdaderos hombres, "real men" as the Spanish liked to call them.

Around the entryway John Lourdes picked up on runs of conversation flush with panic. There were reports alleging Madero, the duly elected president forced into exile by Díaz and living in the United States, was about to declare himself president pro tem and issue a decree for the overthrow of the government. This was fed by rumors rebel armies were already forming to the west in Sonora and Chihuahua to the south. And from the way small armed bands of peons could be seen riding the roads, this had more than just the feel of a rumor. One thing was for certain, Ciudad Juárez would be put under siege. The war would be brought to the border of the United States, for the United States was the world. And U.S. companies, along with British companies, controlled near all the wealth from oil and mining in Mexico.

Rawbone kept on through the crowd, but John Lourdes had stopped at the Customs House entryway. Inside that vaulted lobby booths and tables had been set up by business organizations so concerns could be addressed and pamphlets handed out. On a makeshift stage men took turns speaking from a podium while others waited. Some were met with applause, others excoriation. It was a war of words dedicated to self-proclaimed interests.

Rawbone realized John Lourdes was not with him and went back to the entryway where he stood. "You know what you have here, Mr. Lourdes . . . the practical application of strategy."

Each table had across it a flag naming the organization or association it represented. One read ALLIANCE FOR PROGRESS.

"Mr. Lourdes, this country is gonna burn. So let's get this done and be gone out of here."

91

John Lourdes heard the father well enough, but his mind was turning like the earth as he took dogged inventory of the facts at hand, trying to distill an answer—how one pawn of a truck, moving through a conspiracy of allegiances, meant to affect the world at large.

"Mr. Lourdes?"

The son stared into the Customs House. "This is where we're going," he said.

The father grabbed his arm. "What for?"

"The cause of things."

SIXTEEN

WITH THAT RAWBONE gravely followed. The air in the Customs House was a heady reek of tobacco, nervous sweat and body tonics. John Lourdes led them through a swell of arguments over how these men might best preserve their financial world, till he got close enough to the ALLIANCE FOR PROGRESS table that he could spy unnoticed.

A cadre of businessmen stood around the booth. A flier was being handed out while a poised gentleman, with hands folded and a face near expressionless as a piece of paper, calmly spoke.

"As a member of the American consulate I can speak clearly to the one issue I am constantly asked about. If there is to be a revolution, and it certainly looks as if there will be, what can America do to maintain stability here? Of course, by that you mean, beyond diplomacy, military intervention. Now I know what I'm going to say you don't want to hear, but it's exactly what I have expressed to Mr. Hecht."

The consul looked to the man handing out the fliers in acknowledgment. This Hecht fellow, the one to whom the truck was to be delivered, was old and slightly hunched but had fierce eyes in an otherwise stagnant face.

Rawbone whispered, "He doesn't look much more than a cadaver."

"America is not now, nor should ever be, in the business of nation building," said the consul. "And that is what American military intervention here would mean. It would be a great calamity. And in the end all other nations would stand to reap the advantages, whatever the outcome. And I warn you, our country would end up bearing all the expense only to reap the crop of resulting hatred and revenge unlike anything you could imagine."

The agitated men forced questions but the consul made an officious movement with his hand to signal he was continuing.

"Consider what military intervention would symbolize. What it might foment amongst certain sections of the citizenry. The destruction of the oil fields, the tank farms, the pipelines, the refineries. Do you know what that means in revenues? What the solution is, is open to discussion. What it is not, is—"

A shot registered across that vaulted ceiling. Men scattered from around the stage where a verdadero hombre now stood behind the podium with a smoking revolver he used as a gavel. He had a formal and very charged face, with a mustache grown to the shores of his chin line, and he spoke in the crude but poetic Spanish of a rural hacendado.

"I've come all the way from the south. I listen and I listen before I speak. But I speak. You think with your pockets. Sadly. But you know what is between your pockets." He stood away from the platform. The gun hung from one hand and with the other he grabbed his crotch. There was a wall of laughter and applause that he waved away with his revolver.

"You know what else is between your pockets." He touched his heart reverently. "And this also." He then touched his head. "What are the right principles? Our people live to be only thirty. Most are in homes that are uninhabitable. Because you are all only of the pockets. God on high is watching. And God on high is taking measure of your souls. I've come all the way from the south to tell you this."

A squad of customs guards responding to the shot now appeared. They drove through the crowd in a phalanx of rifles toward the man on the stage with the gun who was speaking to that crowd, near yelling. "I am not finished yet . . . I have one thing more to say before I am taken by the wolves."

His arm swung toward the soldiers and Rawbone had to pull John Lourdes back or he would have been driven under by a rush of boots and bayonets. And then, of all things, it was the crowd around the stage that refused the soldiers a pathway. These businessmen and merchants, these signposts for a kind of strangled masculinity, once in the presence of a true verdadero hombre, wanted to prove their mettle, at least for a few minutes. And so the speaker continued.

"It was God at his most blessed who gave you this." He touched his head. "So you would know what is right. It was God at his most blessed who gave you this." And he touched his heart. "So you could feel what is right. And it was God who gave you these," he grabbed his crotch again, "so you would have the fuckin' cojones to do what is right even if it means your own death. That is God's holy trinity on earth. And if you do not live by that you are just useless pockets—"

He'd barely gotten out the last word when the customs guards on an order surged and took the stage. The hombre belted his weapon and put up no resistance and a pathway of retreating bodies opened and he was shuttled out and the pathway closed and he was gone almost before his words fell silent. Then it was as if he had never been there at all.

John Lourdes bent down to pick up a couple of ALLIANCE FOR PROGRESS fliers that had fallen to the floor. They were about a fund drive and petition signing to rally support for American intervention in case of war.

As he stood Rawbone said, "There's only one thing missing in this place, and you know what it is . . . the headstones, Mr. Lourdes, the headstones."

"Come with me."

"Too staunchly orthodox to appreciate the humor in it?"

John Lourdes looked for a quiet place along the far wall. One thing he could say about what he'd seen of the evening so far, it was as if they'd stumbled upon a well-defended and determined institution whose charter read, "Justice is secondary; security is the byword."

He took out his notepad.

"Do you take down anything I say, Mr. Lourdes? For posterity, I mean."

He handed Rawbone one of Merrill's business cards and the pencil. "Write Anthony Hecht . . . Alliance for Progress . . . and the address."

He turned so the father could use his back. Rawbone placed the card there and did as he was commanded. Still, he wanted to know, "Why am I doing this? I can see the bastard from here. I know the address. It's just a matter of me delivering the truck."

John Lourdes turned. "There's been a change of plans. You're not delivering the truck."

"What the hell is going on in your head?"

The son pointed over the father's shoulder and he turned to see. The walls of the Customs House had been decorated with murals. The one they stood beneath was of a Christ somewhere in the Mexican desert, ministering to two angels.

"And I thought you didn't have a sense of humor. Well, shame on me, Mr. Lourdes."

SEVENTEEN

ANTHONY HECHT HAD no idea whatsoever about this unshaved and slightly filthy rough calling him by name. Looking at a business card held up like a cigarillo between two fingers told him even less.

Hecht took the card. Saw what was scribbled on the back. He had been in dialogue with the consul and excused himself.

"You are?"

"Rawbone, Mr. Hecht."

"And the card means to me?"

"I saw Merrill two days ago outside El Paso. He told me to meet him here. Introduce myself to you. Said there might be some work for me with him."

"Two days? Where again?"

"A roadhouse near Fort Bliss. He was with a couple of gents."

The old man rubbed his lower lip with the tip of his finger. Was that worry or doubt in those fierce old eyes?

"How do you know James?"

Rawbone laughed. "You ever see that photo he carries in his wallet? Manila Harbor. The China. Him and members of his squad. The one on the far right is yours truly. 'Course I was younger." He winked. "And more brash."

He could see the old man was taking the trap. "Is Merrill back?" he asked.

"He is not."

"Oh," said Rawbone. He'd edged the word in disappointment. Then, with a hint of worry himself, said, "I thought he would be."

"I thought he would be, too."

The son watched the two men from the street. They might look like a curious pair, but stripped down, the son had a feeling they were brothers of necessity. The talking went on for a while, though it was mostly Rawbone, who seemed appropriately toned down and serious. The son-of-a-bitch even got to the point where he was showing Hecht the automatic he carried in his belt, the old man regarding it deferentially.

THE BOY FOUND Anthony Hecht easily enough. He had been working the Customs House rally with a gang of other boys, running to get buggies for tips, sprinting to the tobacconist or the saloon around the corner for beer and liquor.

"I was asked to deliver this to you, sir." He held out one of the ALLIANCE FOR PROGRESS fliers. It had been folded in half.

Rawbone watched as the old man read. The shill was being applied to him alright, and hard. Hecht's eyes grew enormous and wild, and that but for an instant, otherwise the old man was as self-contained as a can of processed meat.

"Who asked you to deliver this?"

"A fella outside."

Hecht followed the boy as best he could, but he was already amongst the night crowd on the sidewalk when Hecht caught up with him.

"He was here," said the boy.

"Was he driving a truck?"

"No. He was standing here. And he pointed at you."

JOHN LOURDES WALKED back to the funeraria to wait. It was quiet when he arrived. Upstairs was an apartment. Panes of light emanated from the adobe walls where a hulking shadow leaned into the porch railing above. It was McManus. He called for John Lourdes to come upstairs.

The apartment was filthy. Wash hung from a line in an area by the stove. A near-hairless mongrel drank from drip puddles that had accumulated on the floor. There were reels of film everywhere. An old ratty couch was literally buried under them. McManus sat at a table strewn with beer bottles. He was rolling what looked to be a cigarette when he told John Lourdes to sit and steal himself a Single X.

Rolling that cigarette with just one hand, he was dexterous as some dancing fancy. "You were asking about the Alliance for Progress and Anthony Hecht." He licked the paper closed and pointed it at a reel of film lying on the table. "I've got something to run up on the projector. If you find it valuable, maybe you'll toss a little extra goodwill my way."

John Lourdes thumbed open the beer cap. "Why not." He drank. "It's not my goodwill I'll be handing out."

McManus raised his prosthesis with its oddly spread fingers. "There we go."

"You lose your arm in the war?"

McManus lit up, and when John Lourdes got a scent of that tobacco he knew what it was. McManus offered the young man a draw.

"I'll stick with the beer."

"Too bad Rawbone's not here. He's partial to the reefer. It's a little something we all picked up in Manila, besides the clap." McManus set the cigarette down on the edge of the table. He reached inside his stained shirt and pulled out a necklace. Resting in his palm was this enormous snow-white human front tooth, root and all.

"I got into a stupid fight with a stupider drunk. I hit him so hard his tooth embedded in the bone of my middle knuckle. Right to the root it went. The fool must have had rabies or something 'cause I got an infection and the arm had to come off. I wear it to remember—don't never do anything stupid."

He slipped the cigarette in his mouth and stood. He tucked the reel of film up under his arm. "Let's go see about some goodwill."

McManus threaded the projector in the dark. A charge of smoky light shot past where John Lourdes stood. Out of the dark a world opened. He was suddenly a traveler on the Gulf Coast of Mexico. From a sandy ridgetop a vast panorama of oil fields. Moments cut from one to the next—plumes of charred air rising from refineries, a legion of worker huts, a train moving off into a seared wasteland.

"These are newsreels President Díaz had filmed to show off the country. Prosperity and publicity. But mostly they're about him."

He held the cigarette near his nose and snorted in the smoke. "I like the world better in black and white. It seems closer to the soul of things that way. What say you, Mr. Lourdes?"

The scene shifted again. El Presidente in all his aging pomp and splendor was flanked by an array of dignitaries and businessmen and generals. He stood with hand on saber gesturing for the viewer to come and witness for himself a burgeoning world.

The camera cut from oil-soaked men at a huge derrick to an army of laborers constructing a pipeline to a tanker waiting at sea. The men smiled for the camera, but they were a poor, tired lot.

It was when the entourage with the president began to move that John Lourdes noticed Anthony Hecht. And who should be there just back and behind him?

The scene shifted again and John Lourdes asked, "Can you stop the film. And go back. Just, I saw someone."

The moment froze. The screen went white. McManus reeled back the film and as the scenes replayed John Lourdes stepped into the light and his arm's shadow reached out to point. "There's Anthony Hecht. Do you know him?"

"Only by name . . . Alliance for Progress."

"And that man. Just behind him. Do you know him?"

"I do not."

"Ever seen him?"

"I have not. Who is it?"

"James Merrill."

In the film, Hecht leaned around and said something to Merrill, who nodded. As they moved past the camera, another man was revealed with Merrill.

Only this was no ordinary man. He had a nighthawk face that seemed at odds with his snowy white hair and mustache. He wore a gray suit and, in fact, was rather young. Somewhere in age between Rawbone and John Lourdes.

"I know the one with Merrill," said McManus. "The white-haired fellow."

John Lourdes studied the man on film. He walked with his hands folded behind his back. He was polished and erect and he moved with an economy of motion and gesture.

"He used to be a Texas Ranger. College-educated. Washington, or a place like that. Was a professor before. Doctor Stallings is how he's called."

The last of the film rattlesnaked through the sprockets. John Lourdes disappeared somewhere in that empty screen chasing yet what he did not know.

"The Ranger . . . what does he do now?"

"Private security."

McManus turned off the projector. The room went dark.

Sometimes there is only the vague outline of a thing moving through an uncharted obscurity. What John Lourdes had suddenly was a sense of pure exhilaration he was hunting down a truth that would hold all this together. Yet, he also experienced a sense of pure dread. It seemed unremitting and without cause, but it was there.

When light from the doorway fell long upon that room John Lourdes saw he and McManus were not alone. The little man who'd been sleeping on the desk who Rawbone had roughed up entered and was carrying a shotgun. He made a wide berth around both men, keeping close to the wall. Where he was pointing those double black barrels was clear.

EIGHTEEN

"**E**MMANUEL, I'M GOING to relieve Mr. Lourdes of his weapon."
McManus eased around John Lourdes and with a meaty grip lifted the automatic with slow care. He then slid it down into his belt.

He went to the projector and picked up the cigarette and took another long hit of smoke and placed it back down. His eyes got watery and he grinned a bit. He began to rethread the film through the projector.

"We're gonna see this newsreel again and you'll explain about these people and what you're doing here and why there's a truckload of weapons in my garage."

"What you're doing is ill advised."

"Is it! Well . . . I smoked this marijuana just to keep me eased up. 'Cause I'm prone . . . that's why I told you the tooth story. Oh, and that notebook of yours. Put it on the bench there."

As he reached into his pocket, John Lourdes shot a cursory glance at Emmanuel that McManus caught. He finished threading the film, then walked over to the bench. He shook his head in coarse disappointment over John Lourdes. He picked up the notebook and in the same breath of motion brought his prosthesis down like a bludgeon across the side of John Lourdes's head.

The force drove John Lourdes back over the bench and he hit the floor with a ferocious groan. The room and everything about it were pure liquid. He struggled over onto his shoulder and tried to rise. He saw he was leaving splotches of blood on the wood slats.

McManus set the notebook in the palm of his wooden hand and thumbed pages with the other. John Lourdes used a bench to get to his knees. Blood from a laceration at the corner of one eye left a dripping red track down the side of his face. McManus remained impassive, reading page after page, while Emmanuel stood watch by the wall with the shotgun bearing down on John Lourdes. He was trying to collect himself when from that downturned face the eyes of McManus rose and they were telling.

"I see BOI written down here everywhere."

"This has nothing to do with you."

He took the notebook with his good hand. His great chest slowly expanded. "A friend and me used to rob homes in San Francisco. I was watch; he was the window jockey. We robbed this woman once who was a piano player. This was her arm, that's why it's too short. And why the thumb and pinky," he held out the prosthesis, "are so spread apart. So she could hit the keys." He made like he was actually playing. "It was built by a gent in Northampton, England." He turned his wrist as if John Lourdes might like to see where it had been engraved. "It makes a fine club. But nothing compared to what I got here in my pocket."

He wedged the notebook between two prosthetic fingers. With his good hand he removed a short and shiny black billy stick. He slipped his hand through the rawhide strap. He started toward John Lourdes and let it hang down at his thigh so he could get a good look at it. Standing over him, McManus asked, "Does Rawbone know you're with the BOI?"

John Lourdes did not answer and the billy came down on his kidney. There was a blinding charge of pain up his back. He was asked again, and again his answer was silence. He was clinging to the bench with one elbow when he heard a whoosh of air. The next blow landed with flawless accuracy. A tide of bile came up into his mouth, but his mind was curiously clear.

"Does he know?"

John Lourdes's head hung down as he tried to wrench himself upright.

"Does he know?"

"Why don't you ask me yourself?"

Rawbone stood in the doorway with derby in hand, a burner of light behind his shadowed features.

"He's with the BOI," said McManus.

Rawbone entered the room, approaching so Emmanuel and that shotgun were always within his field of vision. He spoke directly to John Lourdes. "It looks like you didn't do as I told you back at the Mills Building. Where to keep those eyes."

The son picked up the leading tone in the father's voice and with a slight turn of body saw Rawbone had his pocket automatic concealed in the derby.

"Did you know he was with the BOI?"

"Of course, I knew."

"And you brought him into my life?"

"This has nothing to do with your life. And there was money for you in it."

"You lied to me about him."

"I thought it was the most practical solution, knowing you."

McManus flung the notebook at the father. It hit his face and landed on the wood floor near the son.

"You're a shill now for the BOI."

John Lourdes reached for the notebook. He gripped the bench to stand. Rawbone helped to get him upright.

"That's right. Get him up, dust him off. You're a Goddamn butler. A manservant."

The father looked the son over to see how bad the beating was. "By the way, Mr. Lourdes, you've had some luck tonight."

The son, at that moment, was not so sure.

"Your note. It had the effect on Mr. Hecht you wanted."

John Lourdes nodded and wiped at the blood that was running down his face and neck. "Pay your friend what it's worth. And let's get from here."

"What do you want?"

McManus turned his attention to Rawbone. "What have you become?"

"I'll need my gun back," said John Lourdes.

McManus disregarded him. "What have you become?" he repeated.

"Call your fee," said Rawbone.

McManus ordered, "Emmanuel."

The little man with the shotgun took a step forward, kicking away a bench that was in his path.

"I said, what have you become?"

"Don't do this," said Rawbone.

"What have you become?"

There was a furied determination to McManus about having that question answered. The son studied the father; he noted the slightest movement of the hand with the derby.

"We've been friends, how long?" said Rawbone.

"Answer."

"Alright. I came to this place as some would say, a common as-sassin. And I'll be leaving this place the same way. So now . . . what's your fee?"

"What have you become?"

"Jesus, man. It's about survival, alright. My personal survival. And I don't want to hear you keep talking from the belt buckle down. What's your fee?"

"McManus!" shouted John Lourdes. "The BOI wants nothing with you."

McManus leaned into Rawbone and looked down at him and said, "You're the hole in the shithouse floor now."

"What's your fee?"

"There's more than survival."

"So you say. Now what's your fee?"

The man's head lolled to one side like a great bear, slowly, and the eyes grew small as vapor drops. "You're my fee."

"Aye, brother," said Rawbone. And just like that, before his derby hit the floor, he had wheeled about and fired his automatic repeatedly. The little man named Emmanuel had no business being behind a shot-gun. He was driven back and crying out, jerked in half. The shotgun went off wildly. A gas lamp exploded, throwing stars of glass and sparks everywhere. The funeral drapes on the far wall were run with flames.

Before Rawbone could turn McManus plowed that slagheap of a body right at him and got a grip on his gun hand. He kept right on for the wall, churning his legs with Rawbone trying to break loose and the gun going off wildly. John Lourdes locked his arms around McManus's neck to pull him back, but he was too strong and using his shoulder flung the young man like he was nothing against the projector. The motor kicked on and there was the click, click, click, click, click, click of the turning sprockets and a rush of dusty light and Rawbone was battered right into the adobe.

An ugly sound came out of Rawbone as if he'd been staved clear through. He'd expended all his ammunition. The body of the dead Emmanuel lay a foot away. The shotgun angled upright across his corpse. Rawbone twisted and bent to try and get low enough to reach the weapon. John Lourdes again was right on McManus, this time bracing his arms up under the dense shoulders to pull him loose. McManus lost his footing briefly and Rawbone was able to score himself down the wall just enough for his fingers to crab around the barrel and take hold before McManus righted himself.

McManus began to yell out a pained and atavistic war cry. He used his prosthesis like a whip but he had Rawbone still in the clench of his one good arm and there wasn't enough space for a breath between them. The three were all tangled together now and they spun crazily, crashing over benches. The newsreel began to play and their shadows wraithed across the screen where President Díaz stood before an array of businessmen and dignitaries and generals and invited the viewer to come and see a burgeoning world.

The smoke from the drapes afire grayed the air. McManus now struggled backward. His boots clopped out a sidling but steady drum of steps. He was like a freight car to take down and the two men even together could not. Rawbone still had the shotgun in his grasp, working to edge his fingers down the barrel.

The three were entwined like some ancient statue from the shores of Troy within the light of the screen and across their bodies were flickering images of vast petrol fields on the Gulf and oil-slicked men with their tired faces and a lone train moving toward blanched and serrated mountains.

The drapes were a mural of smolder and flame. The men grunted like animals for each gasp of air. McManus now steadied himself and slammed John Lourdes against the adobe. He then leaned forward and the young man's boots scruffed along the wood. McManus slammed back again and the blood from the wound above John Lourdes's eye spattered over the side of McManus's face.

Rawbone gasped, "Mr. Lourdes, can you hold my friend a bit longer?"

"I can . . . hold."

And now Rawbone drove the top of his head into that spur of a chin as he worked his hand down to the trigger. And John Lourdes got an arm around that bear of a head to wrench it back. And Rawbone snaked and squeezed his other arm across his body and finally he steadied up the weapon. McManus watched the barrel clock out inches till it was no longer if, but when.

Rawbone, near wasted with exhaustion, said, "Let it go."

McManus would not have it.

"Just give up and we'll be done with this."

McManus opened his mouth and hissed.

"To what end?"

Rawbone confronted a harpoon stare.

"Mr. Lourdes, force your head back."

John Lourdes bent away as best he could.

"Friend," said Rawbone, "let it go or you'll be this moment forever."

The face above the gun barrel filled with floodwaters of defiance and contempt and a reverie to fearlessness and in the smoke and sweep of images flickering on the screen the moment saw Rawbone pull the trigger.

NINETEEN

HE FACE WAS there one moment, and the next it was a denuded mass of bone and blood. That great hull of muscle and will dropped like a boulder to the floor. Rawbone stood with smoke and strips of burning cloth floating in the air about him, looking down at what was his friend. "All he had to do was let it go."

John Lourdes knelt exhausted and choking from the smoke. He rolled the body over and tugged his automatic from the dead man's belt. He stood. Rawbone was still staring down at the brutal evidence of what just had happened.

"Put the fire out," said John Lourdes.

"Leave it—"

The last of the film kite tailed with the endless turning of the reel as John Lourdes looked over the projector.

"What are you doing?"

"Put the fire out."

JOHN LOURDES WALKED out of the funeraria and into a star-filled night with the reel of film under his arm. It was quiet, save for the lone wail of a distant train. Rawbone stood looking across the river and smoking when he joined him. The father took a bandana from his back pocket and handed it to the son. "You're still leaking oil."

Rawbone went back to looking across the river. His past loomed out there in the dark. He was heir to the brazen hand of his own making, and he knew it. John Lourdes watched. Rawbone seemed distant and troubled, and caught up in a strained uncertainty. It was a picture of the man the son did not remember as a boy. Of course, it could well have been the part a boy could not recognize.

"He flat out perished himself," said Rawbone. "Why?"

The son was not sure the father expected him to answer. He had a sense of why, but his was an emotional verdict he meant to use at the appropriate time, with a vengeance.

Rawbone pointed to the reel of film. "What's so important about that?"

John Lourdes explained about the film and how he thought it might prove to be evidence connecting certain people and events. Rawbone offered a clipped and sarcastic laugh. "I guess the future will come in all shapes and surprises." Then he took from his pocket a slip of notepad paper and pencil the son had given him.

"Like I said before, Mr. Lourdes. You had some good luck tonight." He passed the notepaper and pencil to the son. "And your good luck tonight is my good fortune tomorrow."

The father was animated now and near grinning. "Tomorrow you'll be Justice Knox's sainted poker hand of an agent and I'll be pleasantly off for parts unknown." To that he added, "With a clear conscience and a clean record."

Rawbone was able to cast aside what had just happened with absolute impunity and refocus on himself. It was a trait, though not noble, John Lourdes thought he'd better acquire.

He looked at the father's chicken-scratch handwriting. He saw names—the word railroad, underlined a number of times—and the Panuco River.

Rawbone described how the scam to get him into Hecht's good graces had played out even better than he could have imagined. And the note John Lourdes had written—

As they walked to the warehouse behind the funeraria Rawbone near mocked a reading of it: "Mr. Hecht, I've arrived with the makings of your icehouse—Will arrange for financial settlement tomorrow morning."

Each took a shed door to open. The hinges groaning as they went. Rawbone kept on, "It was a priceless way to word it, Mr. Lourdes. That note was delivered all the way up to the headwaters of his asshole."

Rawbone used his cigarette to wick up a lantern. Light filled that belly of a space and there was the truck, parked beside a hearse that was comely and elegant and covered with dust. The light rivered across its glass casement.

The father went on about the meeting with Hecht as John Lourdes, exhausted and still bleeding, put the reel of film on the cab seat then sat down on the runner.

Rawbone told how Hecht lived in a row house up from Customs. He'd invited the father along, believing him to be a friend of Merrill's. He'd been taken to the kitchen where the cook, an old Mexican woman, was told to offer him food and coffee. Then Hecht excused himself.

Men kept arriving, one and two at a time. There were what sounded like discussions in a far room. The voices were gray and controlled. What he wrote down was all he could pick up under the watchful eye of the cook. He carefully plied her with a few questions, but she was immune to either friendliness or flattery.

When the men left and all was quiet, Hecht returned to the kitchen and excused the cook. The two men had sat like old friends at an ornate table, drinking coffee spiked with gentleman's whiskey.

"He was all polite and full of shit," said Rawbone. "Poking me with questions to size me up. He's a wily bastard." The father looked at himself in the dusty glass paneling of the hearse. His image imprinted there on a glowy lantern dusk. He spoke to himself as if he were Hecht.

"I've to set an arrangement tomorrow to pick up a truck with the makings of an icehouse that is to be delivered south of the city. I was to entrust Merrill the job, but since he is not here and you are a friend . . . and I say to him while I'm filling my cup with more of his gentleman's whiskey . . . 'When Mr. Merrill comes back he'll tell you how I can be trusted, for no one knows me better than he.' Of course, Mr. Hecht has no idea the last I seen Merrill he was leaking oil out of his skull."

Rawbone turned to John Lourdes. "And then he baits me out even better. He says if I do right there'll be a job for me with the men who work with Merrill. Now, Mr. Lourdes, do you see the whole play from his side?"

The father drew down on his cigarette and waited as the son made a silent catwalk through the dark corners of human motive. He'd been holding the bandana to the wound along his eye but now he stood. He looked into the hearse glass to see if the blood had stanched. Rawbone was beside him now. He noted the son beginning to smile and then outright laugh.

"He's throwing you to the wolves."

"There you go. I get the truck, I come back, alright. But if there's chicanery I'm the perfect ignorant fool who ends up in a ditch somewhere."

He put his hand on John Lourdes's shoulder and leaned in to talk as if they were lifers conjoined in criminal plans. "Now, let me tell you how I think we play this out and finish it."

"I can see what you're thinking as far away as forever."

"Is that so?"

"You bring the truck back," said John Lourdes, "and you keep the money. In return you'll deliver it for Hecht but I find out through you where and to whom. Then I go home and you, maybe you take Hecht up on that job. As you say, with a smile and good cheer. You know, you may have accidentally stumbled on a future down here."

"Ah, Mr. Lourdes, you can be a racehorse son-of-a-bitch."

"A pure thoroughbred."

But the son wasn't done yet. He took the cigarette from the father. His mood locked down as he considered a more daggered attack. "You're going to deliver the truck," he said. "But what if you brought a body back with it. To show you had to kill for the truck."

The father drew in closer and eyed the son through the dusty paneling of glass from where he stared back.

"Even the money should have blood on it," said John Lourdes. "Think how much trust you'd have earned. How indebted Hecht would be to you."

In the half shadows of the warehouse the father raised an eyebrow. "A man who can breathe a thought like that has to have a black mark in his life somewhere."

"You have no idea."

Reflection to reflection. The father now cocky and self-possessed. "There's a notion that a hearse should never be cleaned or repaired unless it has a firm booking. Otherwise, if it is readied, it will find itself work. Are you superstitious?"

"No."

"Well, I am. So keep your damn hands clear of it."

RAWBONE WAS SITTING at the kitchen table just as he had the night before, when the phone rang down a hallway. Mr. Hecht entered the room a few minutes later and excused the cook. He had written down the appointed place, the appointed time. He was carrying a leather packet which he set on the table before Rawbone.

West of Calle de la Paz was a ravine that ran all the way to the Rio Bravo. It was also where garbage was dumped. Hours later Rawbone left an urgent message by phone for Hecht to meet him there.

Gulls drifted on the thermals or picked away at the trash. Rawbone smoked and waited alone as a single vehicle struggled its way down that worthless stretch of road.

Mr. Hecht was alone. He looked Rawbone over as he got out of the car. He looked the truck over. "I don't understand," he said. "Why are we here?"

"I'll show you why."

Hecht was led to the rear of the truck, where a tarp was pulled back just enough for him to view what remained of McManus. The old man kept his head at the sight. The leather packet was positioned beside the body. Rawbone held it for Hecht to take. It was blood-stained.

"This one had a different idea about the transaction than you did."

Mr. Hecht waved away the packet.

"THERE'S NOTHING LIKE a finely worked 'fuck you,'" said Rawbone. He removed a thin band of hundreds from the packet, then tossed it aside and pocketed the money.

John Lourdes had watched everything from a stand of trees, join-
ing the father only after the dust trailing Hecht's vehicle had passed
away. He was looking over a note Hecht had written on his personal
stationery. Addressed to a Doctor Stallings, it was about a job and was
to be brought to a railroad siding at the junction of the road to Casas
Grandes.

"You know who the doctor is, don't you?" asked Rawbone.

"I do. He's in that film."

The father put out a hand to shake, but the son was preoccupied
with that letter. "Mr. Lourdes, you have fulfilled your obligation and I,
mine. It is time we part ways."

The son looked up. He did not take the father's hand. "I'm sure
you feel we're both the richer for our time together . . . but we're not
near done yet."

TWENTY

RAWBONE STOOD IN the wind with gulls sweeping overhead and stared at the son as if a mountain had dropped down on him from heaven.

"You better just enlighten me to what you meant."

"You speak the same language I do. We are done only when I say we are done."

"Are you trying to roll me into a ditch?"

He grabbed the letter and started to walk away.

"Where are you going?" said John Lourdes. "Not back."

The father held up the letter. "I'm gonna go get introduced to my future."

By the time Rawbone reached the truck John Lourdes had drawn up behind him with his weapon pressed against the back of the father's neck. With that he stretched his arm and took the automatic Rawbone carried.

John Lourdes stood back. He pointed to the rear of the truck. "McManus . . . you killed him. I know and Mr. Hecht . . . he knows. You might even say he's your accomplice in this. Now if Justice Knox went to Mexican intelligence, well—?"

The son now circled the father. "What you said to me back at the river when you . . . poisoned . . . those three customs agents. 'Mr. Lourdes,' you said, 'it's a means of holding you to the cross.'" There was a flicker of dark accomplishment in his eyes. "We're done only when I say we're done."

"Back there on the street," said Rawbone. "When we were walking to the Customs House and you had that photo. And the note to Hecht. You were plotting then."

"This moment here?"

"This moment here."

As if mocking the father, he said, "Aye. Something pretty close, anyway."

"It does seem like you're a couple of steps up from Montgomery Ward's."

John Lourdes grabbed the letter. "You're gonna deliver this truck and you're gonna get yourself a job and I'm gonna be right there with you and we're gonna find out where this truck is going and who it's going to and why, if it means driving it all the way—"

"I'll be arm-wrestling death first."

"And who says you aren't? Maybe I dusted off that hearse a little in your honor before we left Juárez."

Rawbone changed his tactic. He took out a cigarette and lit it. He leaned back against the truck, stretching his arms across the hood as if he were one broad tendon. "I think I'll just relax here and enjoy the view."

"Listen to me now," said John Lourdes. "I'm not some empty street you're going to walk down and be done with. There is you, there is me, and there is that truck. And that's all. There's no past, there's no future. There is only now. Do you understand?" He pointed his gun at the truck. "That is our world. See the writing there on the side— AMERICAN PARTHENON—that's our world. Nothing else. You . . . me . . . and this truck. And we're going to drive through to the end . . . together. Wherever that end is. Till all that's left are our bones and a chassis, if need be." He was near out of breath and he could feel his whole body in every branched vein running with rage.

He fought to calm himself. "And when we're done. When I see we're done, then you'll have your immunity. Now . . ." He started toward the back of the truck. "Help get Mr. McManus off the truck and to somewhere more . . . befitting his present station."

"What is this really about, Mr. Lourdes?"

The son stopped. His head and shoulders tightened down. He turned.

"Maybe it's that black spot you're carrying around. Or maybe you're desperate to prove what you're not. The ladder is always taller for the small man."

"The teachings of a common assassin."

"I've survived this long because there's legitimacy to me." Rawbone walked to the cab for his bindle. "And what this is really about . . . is the practical application of strategy. As seen through the eyes of one John Lourdes."

Rawbone slung the bindle over one shoulder. He took to walking away. The son saw him and called out, "You think you're leaving but you're not."

The father kept on.

"What about your family?"

Rawbone stopped. His face drained of expression. The son had heard himself say the words but there was no thought to them, no preparation, nor plan. They came out as squalls of pure anger, fully formed. Ready, willing and able to draw blood and serve a purpose at the same time.

"You do have a family, don't you?"

Rawbone flicked away his cigarette.

"In El Paso?"

The father did not move. He only swung the bindle up on his shoulder as if he were getting ready to start away.

"Could it be those questions you were asking of me at the church about the barrio, and did I know families there—"

"I have no idea where you're going," said Rawbone. "But I'll send you my regrets once you get there."

John Lourdes approached, his weapon in one hand, the father's in the other. Both were barreled to the ground.

"What if I told you someone at BOI knows of your family. I might even say Justice Knox has spoken to a member of your family. Would it mean anything to you?"

The son could see something incubating in the eyes and the jawline of the man before him. I have put the knife to him, thought the son. I have found a place that bleeds. Thank God.

"Take a look out there," said John Lourdes.

He meant the ravine so lined with trash along that runnelled pathway that ran with water when the season warranted.

"That's your life." He slapped Rawbone on the back. "And you know what else? When it's your time, McManus will be out here waiting on you. With his wooden arm and marijuana." He even pretended he was banging away one-armed on the ivory keys with those oddly splayed fingers.

Rawbone stood in hard silence watching the display. Then he said, "Mr. Lourdes, I believe I'm going to kill you."

"You mean you're not sure."

John Lourdes took Rawbone's weapon and stuffed it into the front of his trousers. "Now," he said. "You've at least got something between your pockets." He started toward the truck. "I'm going to find Mr. McManus a good spot to watch the sunset."

The father did nothing. He'd been caught off guard and he now evaluated his situation thoughtfully. He looked up that ravine. From Juárez came a carreta pulled by a mule. An old man sat in the box seat. A boy ran alongside, sifting through the trash, holding items he thought valuable aloft and every now and then the old man would nod and wave, yes, yes, and the boy would run to him with an air of pride and achievement at his discovery.

The father removed his derby and wiped at the sweat on the inside brim with his bandana, the one he'd given the son to hold against his wound.

He should have taken his own advice back there on the road to El Paso when he first had the truck. He should have heeded Burr. He should disappear now into a landscape more hostile and befitting his station. Pay intelligent attention to what your insides tell you, for they are ever true. Yet even so—

He set the derby back on his head all cocked and rugged, then called out in that tone of voice he was best known for, "Mr. Lourdes . . . save a seat in the truck for me!"

PART II

TWENTY-ONE

THE ROAD TO Casas Grandes lay to the south. The father drove to occupy his time; the son fought to keep at bay the rising pain from the beating with the black stick that the road made all the more merciless. When he stopped to urinate, the dust around his boots ran wet with red.

"McManus knew his trade," said the father. "You'll be fine in a day or two. Or you won't."

They drove on in the shadow of barren mountains and the son came to see and understand they were being stripped down, mile after mile, one as much as the other, till there would be nothing left between them but who they truly were.

Out of nowhere the father said, "Hammer and anvil. Each will have its turn."

THEY FOLLOWED THE line of the rail tracks for hours and finally came upon Spartan columns of smoke rising above a stand of cottonwoods clinging to the banks of a sorry creek. The siding that was their destination came complete with water tower and warehouses and a repair shed for locomotives.

Approaching the river, they could see through the trees a camp had been established with well over a hundred men. Two trains were being outfitted for a journey. Spanning the narrow river was a slat bridge that had been retrussed to support the weight of trucks with cargo. A couple of wretched-looking gringos on the far side flagged them to stop. When asked their business, Rawbone handed over Hecht's note. One of them read it using a finger on each word before passing it back. He pointed with a filthy hand toward a campaign tent that had been set up in the dry grass beside where the trains were being readied. They would find Doctor Stallings there.

It was a formidable collection of ruffians they encountered driving through the camp and looking over those trains left no uncertainty wherever this expedition was going would be a long way and one should expect violence. The first train had a 0-6-0 locomotive and tender and an open coal car that was out front. The interior of the coal car was being rigged with a shooting platform. The second train had an imposing 4-8-0 Mastodon. That's what the son said the locomotive was named, as he had worked on them at the railyard in El Paso. Built for pulling heavy freight over mountains like the Sierra Madres, it would haul two passenger cars behind the tender, a boxcar after that for mounts, then three flatcars where tanker trucks were being hoisted up and lashed down and lastly another passenger car.

A campaign tent had been set up beside the last car, where about two dozen Mexican women were preparing a meal and setting it out on long tables.

Rawbone downshifted as he pulled up to the tent. The flap was pushed aside and stepping out into the hard daylight was the man John Lourdes had viewed in that flickering newsreel the night before at the funeraria.

Doctor Stallings was recently shaved and neatly attired in a gray suit. Behind him were a pair of security bulls and a young shark brandishing an army gunbelt. His shirtsleeves were cut to the shoulders and one of his arms was tattooed from the wrist all the way to the bladebone with the stars and stripes of the nation.

Before Rawbone shut off the engine, he said under his breath, "Quite a menagerie, hey, Mr. Lourdes."

Doctor Stallings approached the truck. He looked it over with patient care. He saw AMERICAN PARTHENON painted on the side. He was handed the letter. Stallings took it, yet now seemed inordinately curious about the father. He read the letter, then began to walk about the truck. When he was all the way around back, he called out, "The motorcycle . . . whose is it?"

Father and son looked to each other. What to answer? Rawbone was quicker. "It was with the truck when we retrieved it."

Stallings walked up the far side of the vehicle, his hands behind his back, checking the crates, the truck itself. Reaching the cab, he glanced at John Lourdes, but his attention went immediately to the other.

"I feel as if I know you, sir."

Rawbone leaned on the wheel.

"I have an extraordinary facility for faces. Even if they are not particularly interesting or aberrant."

"I believe we've done a round or two in Texas, if that's what you mean."

"Name?"

"Rawbone."

The Doctor's eyes rose and his mouth made a silent ahhh. "The letter refers to you." He jutted his chin toward John Lourdes. "What is this one about?"

The son went to speak for himself, but the father put out a hand to stop him. He leaned past John Lourdes as if he were not even there and in a very private voice said to Stallings, "Retrieving this truck was no easy matter, as Mr. Hecht can personally validate. And well, this young man may have that Montgomery Ward's look, but if it wasn't for him . . . I wouldn't be here right now."

The son picked up the acid mischief in the voice aimed at him and then the father's glance went from the camp to the train to that crew of thugs by the tent. "Doctor Stallings, in expeditions such as these you are about to embark on, it has been my personal experience there are always . . . casualties."

Doctor Stallings was expressionless. He pocketed the letter and started for the tent. As he did he called out, "Jack B, have the truck with its cargo put on the train. And get both these men security cards . . . after a proper introduction."

Jack B, it turned out, was the young shark with that heavily inked arm. He motioned for the truck to follow. They drove down the length of those waiting cars where men played cards or loafed. On the roof of one, two men posed with their rifles as a young, wiry Mexican took photographs of them with a folding pocket camera.

"It might have been a mistake," John Lourdes said, "to bring the motorcycle. If Merrill and his men left from here the Doctor could have recognized—"

"Of course, he recognized it. Why do you think he asked. And as for bringing it here being a mistake, the mistake is being here at all."

Jack B had them pull up to the hoist and then he told the work crew this truck was going aboard with its loaded cargo. Both men were

then ordered to step down from the cab. As they did the two security
bulls from the tent approached with weapons drawn.

"You're going to be searched now," said Jack B. "Turn about.
You, put your hands on the hood. You, hands on the truckbed."

Both did as they were ordered. The father glanced at the son. At the
pocket where the notebook was tucked away.

Rawbone got his head shoved by a calloused hand into the truck
siding and was told to look forward. His pockets were burrowed into
and a wallet loosed. It had nothing in it save money. John Lourdes's
wallet had no money, but it did have a photo of his mother and the
cross with its chipped-off beam. The father kept trying to steal a look,
edging his head a bit, angling his eyes sidewise. He caught a glint of
sunlight on that crucifix but it didn't register a meaning. This was not
where his ruin lay, or so he thought.

TWENTY-TWO

HE SWEATED OUT that other bull crabbing through the son's pockets, pulling them up and out one by one till they hung there in the daylight. But in the end, the damn notebook was nowhere to be found.

"You can both come around now."

The father eyed the son while he nonchalantly pushed the pockets back in place. Both men were tossed their wallets and personals. Jack B took security cards from his shirt pocket and handed one to each man. John Lourdes looked the card over. Rawbone wasn't the least interested and couldn't get it in his pocket quick enough. The card, as John Lourdes read it:

> AGUA NEGRA
> PRIVATE SECURITY

"The truck is your responsibility. You'll stay on the flatcar with it. You'll sleep there with it. Unless and until you are ordered otherwise."

Jack B was yelling orders now to the hoist crew about the truck when Rawbone asked, "Hey stars and stripes, where's this parade goin'?"

"What does it matter to you?"

Rawbone pushed his derby back and leaned casually against the truck. "If I knew I could write my dear old mom and tell her what kind of dresses she should send me to wear."

John Lourdes did his best to seem like he had not heard that. Jack B, on the other hand, said, "This ain't Texas."

He walked away to Rawbone whistling "I'm a Yankee Doodle Dandy." Then, the father's attention turned to the son. "The notebook—"

The son strode past the father and leaned down and reached in under the back of the cab. When he stood he had the notebook in his hand. He held it up, then slipped it back in his pocket. He'd hidden it away before they left Juárez as a precaution.

Rawbone leaned over the hood now and called to a roustabout who was carrying over a set of chains to hook to the chassis for lifting the truck. "Hey, gent, where's this parade goin'?"

The man wiped a gloved hand across his heavily bearded chin. "You're here and you don't know?"

"I'm here and I don't know and how much of an offspring of morons does that make me?"

"The Zone, brother. That's where we're bound."

"Aye. Thank you, gent. And be so kind as not to tell anyone you just talked to a buffoon with an empty boot for brains."

"That's our secret, brother."

The father spit. Both men grew quiet. They knew what the Zone meant—oil country. The Gulf Coast from Tampico to Tuxpan.

The Golden Lane is how it was described in newspapers or defined on maps. But if you'd been there and seen, you damn well knew it was an unreckonable sweep of devastation and fires, black rain and poisoned earth. The father had been witness to the place; he'd done time on the streets and in the bars and oil fields of Tampico and Puerto Lobos and Cerro Azul and case-hardened as he was, he wanted none of it. "Next stop, one thousand miles," he said.

"Yeah."

"Talk about a blackened scrap of meat."

John Lourdes wiped at an unusual amount of sweat coming off his forehead.

"Mr. Lourdes—"

"We're going."

"Going does not mean getting there."

"We'll get there."

"Take a look at yourself."

The son wiped at the sweat again.

"You look like a pile of salt sitting out in the noon sun." He pointed his derby at the young man's back. "You're leaking blood, Mr. Lourdes."

The son wiped at his face. He looked around. He walked over to the last passenger car and climbed the steps judiciously. He peered into the door window. Rawbone turned up at his elbow. The sunlight that fell across the window helped tell the story. His face was drained of color alright and the cheeks were close to the look of skimmed ice.

His glance went from himself to the father's, and like the night before in the hearse glass when the two were side by side, there was not even the slightest recognition from the father that a few demarked features of each were so much alike. Maybe the resemblance was too quiet, or some nameless trait inside the man who was Rawbone made such moments impossible. The son grinned and the father grew suddenly uncomfortable.

"I'm bleeding alright. But . . . we're going on. You will not use me, against me."

"Why should I bother, Mr. Lourdes, when you do such an exemplary job on yourself? I'll just stand here and beat the drum."

As they stood and argued the father picked up on a figure stepping from the shadows of the tent. "Mr. Lourdes, I believe you have attracted someone's attention."

With that he angled his head toward where the son should look. There Teresa was, stepping from the tent's shadow. She was with the women and she arced a hand over her eyes to cut off the sunlight and be sure.

He could not fathom it any more than the girl. She put out her hands uncertainly as if to ask what he was doing here. Realizing the danger, he quickly gathered himself and came down the train steps scrambling for his notepad and pencil. He began to write furiously. Then he tore the sheet of paper from the pad and handed it to her: *You must say nothing about who I am, or how you know me. It is important. It might mean my life, if you do. I will explain later.*

Rawbone watched as the girl regarded the note wide-eyed and frightened. She wanted to ask questions, for she pointed to the notepad and pencil and scribbled on the air, but John Lourdes motioned no, and pointed to the word—*later.*

He took the page he'd written on and tore it up as he started back to the train. Climbing the steps, he tossed the pieces in the air. He stood with Rawbone as Teresa was taken in tow by another woman and prodded back to work. John Lourdes was decidedly troubled.

"That wouldn't be the girl you told me about, would it?"

"It would."

"The one whose father you killed?"

"The same."

"Well, I hope she takes the news as well as her father did."

BY LATE AFTERNOON the great Mastodon whistle blew. Along the creek birds struck from the treetops skyward in a frenzy. The battalion of roustabouts and thugs ran along the rail line and jumped the car steps or leapt to the flatbed. The truck had been chained down and braced to the last flatcar.

John Lourdes sat with his back against the cab tire facing the sun, hoping it would ease the chills and fever that were beginning to overcome him. Rawbone stood nearby, arms folded, and watched Doctor Stallings and his committee of security officers pose for a last photo before they embarked. The Mexican with the camera was animated and lively as he posed the men before the steaming wheels of that black monster engine. They then boarded and the photographer ran to the first flatbed and put out a hand and was hauled up with legs kicking wildly.

The boiler chest flooded with steam that entered the cylinders through valve sleeves and the pistons were driven backward and the wheels began to turn. That metal and wood chain of hulls groaned and creaked and steam escaped through the exhaust port and there was a long low huff followed by another and then another and the train labored forward. The trek to the Gulf and what awaited had begun.

TWENTY-THREE

THE PLACE FROM whence they came disappeared in the heat like a mirage. John Lourdes still sat with his back against the cab tire. He was trying to write down all that had transpired since the funeraria, but fever left his hands trembling and eyes unclear. He looked toward the passenger car coupled to the flatbed where all the women traveled together.

He once saw the girl Teresa in the door window like a lonely portrait, watching him. In the paling light she put a hand to the glass and with a finger traced a cross with rays coming from it. He remembered that was what she had written in his notebook that night at the church and he pulled that notebook from his coat pocket and opened to the page and held it for her to see.

The night winds came with the dusk. The men bundled up in their coats to contend with the cold desert dark. The one with the camera was making the rounds from car to car flashing a business card and trying to hustle up commissions. John Lourdes whistled to him and weakly waved the man over his way.

He leapt to the car all lithe and smart. He wasn't much older than John Lourdes and spoke in a blaze of Spanish and sawed-off English and he flashed his business card.

TUERTO

FOTOGRAFIA EXTRAORDINARIA

John Lourdes pointed up to the truck cab. "The gent up there brooding." Tuerto glanced at Rawbone. "He saw you posing Doctor Stallings today and it got him pretty jealous 'cause there's nothing he'd like better than having a photographer primp him while he had his picture taken. I'll even pay for it."

The father, in fact, had been brooding, till Tuerto overwhelmed him with compliments about his verdadero hombre features. It was an inspiring hustle and he let Rawbone handle the folding pocket Kodak. As part of his pitch he began to instruct him on its use. He showed how to open it, explained what the maroon leather bellows was for, demonstrating the metal tool to steady it for longer horizontal exposures.

Tuerto pulled out a deck of Kodak penny postcards. "The newest rage," he said in English. "Take a picture, Kodak will have it printed on a penny postcard. Mail it anywhere in the world, to anyone you want. A loved one, perhaps?"

Rawbone went through each, looking them over as if they were charged relics from the time of Christ. Tuerto explained about how he studied photography in Mexico City and wanted to be a great picture postcard artist. "Tuerto," he said, "means one-eyed." He ran a finger around the single lens opening in the camera's black frontpiece. "Tuerto," he repeated. He had taken it as a sort of nom de plume, for his given name was Manuelito Miguel Tejara Flores.

"If I wanted to get pictures of this train," said John Lourdes, "you could do that?"

"Of course."

"And of the people on it?"

"Of course."

"And you could have them delivered somewhere. El Paso, say. If I gave you an address?"

"Of course."

"And if I wanted to buy from you copies of pictures you'd already taken, could I do that?"

Tuerto thought that a most unusual request.

"He's a most unusual fellow," said Rawbone.

"I guess," said Tuerto, "for a fee."

John Lourdes put his head back and closed his eyes. His head began to swim. "You have been commissioned."

Tuerto thanked both men enthusiastically. Rawbone then climbed down from the cab seat and squatted beside John Lourdes.

"You hustled him."

The son did not open his eyes.

"I'm trying to accumulate information and possible evidence that pertains to this investigation any way I can. So I can go home. And you can earn your immunity."

"That's why you called him over."

"Who told me once to keep my gunsights at eye level?"

Rawbone continued to regard John Lourdes, who without opening his eyes, moved his head slightly.

"You're blocking what little light there is," said the son.

The father remained as he was, clicking his jaw left, then right. Finally he admitted, "There's times, Mr. Lourdes, you've said things. Like to that photographer about me jealous wanting my picture taken. It was like you knew me all my life."

The son opened his eyes. "Or all my life."

"Exact."

His eyes shut now in spite of him. The father continued to block the light and the son shifted a bit more.

"Mr. Lourdes, did you ever have something you wanted to do with your life more than anything else?"

"I'm doing it now."

"Ah. Me . . . if I was your age and could start over, I'd go where they make those moving-picture shows. I would gent up and . . ."

"With a smile and good cheer . . ."

"Goddamn right. That would be me up there."

The son's eyelids fluttered, the pupils now barely visible. The face before him blurred into a landscape where the last of the sun bled away everything before it and the endless clackety-clack of the train wheels became that of the film tailing wildly through the sprockets. The image suddenly fever rushed up of the father as this terrifying wonder in flickering black and white adorned with near heroic indifference to life. He leaned forward shivering horribly and grabbed hold of Rawbone's coat. "Think how you'd . . . be able to . . . help them get . . . the dyin', right." John Lourdes grinned and the father stared down at him confounded and the son grinned yet and tried with a falling voice to sing, "You're a Yankee . . . Doodle . . . Dandy, a—"

And with that he passed out.

Rawbone pulled the son's head back by the hair. "Mr. Lourdes," he said, and then, "son-of-a-bitch," he let the body drop back against the truck tire, then sag over.

"I ought to throw your ass from the train."

RAWBONE APPEARED IN the darkened passenger car doorway, banging on the window. He confronted a huddled wall of faces illuminated by a few candle tips of light as he tried to explain in Spanish about John

Lourdes lying back there on the flatbed and asking for the deaf girl named Teresa.

The women just stared at this intent and hard-faced stranger. He then tried to push the door open, but it had been braced shut and he cursed their Goddamn souls for not moving and told them to open the damn door or he'd put a fist through it.

Teresa watched in confusion from the back of the car till she saw the familiar pocket notebook pressed against the glass. She came forward cautiously and when Rawbone caught sight of her stepping from the motty shadows he motioned as he yelled for her to get the hell over here.

As she read the note the father had written, he pointed to John Lourdes lying unconscious at the edge of the flatbed where Tuerto had dragged him. An owlish crone of a woman came forward and took charge, ordering Rawbone to bring the boy to her.

He jumped the gap between cars and with Tuerto lugged John Lourdes up over his shoulder. He straddled that rattling flatbed like a drunk and readied himself and then jumped over the couplings. One boot missed the landing and were it not for a flock of arms grabbing at him amidst pitched cries both men would have gone under the wheels.

The seats in the car had been torn out. The women had set up blankets and bedding on the floor and Rawbone was told to lay the boy down on one of the dozen or so filthy straw mattresses Stallings had brought onboard. He was then pushed and prodded and shooed down the length of that car cursing their sorry asses as they shut the door on him and braced it. Cupping his hands on the window and looking into that swaying corridor through a current of moving dresses and candles, he managed to get a glimpse of John Lourdes being stripped of his clothes while a small circle of women sat around a patchquilt suitcase. That crone of a woman was removing small pouches from the suitcase and from what he could make out of their sorry birdlike chatter, they were discussing herbs and homegrown medicinals. Then a shawl was draped over the window and he was left staring at black.

HE SAT ON the truck seat, smoking in the dark. A troubled anger cauled his insides as he stared into the swiftly passing desert where hills rose close to the tracks near claustrophobically, only to disappear in the lifetime of a second.

It was not about whether John Lourdes would die or not; for purely selfish reasons he did not want him to die. But if he did, well—

He looked back at the passenger car cradling and pitch dark. Maybe it was the women with their raven hair and Indian faces and poisonous mix of delicacy and strength. Maybe it was the smells that clung to their clothes and hair. Lemon and vanilla, the musk of candlesmoke. Maybe it was the discarded family he should never have Goddamn gone back to El Paso for, as that act had fated him to this forsaken place and hour. These moments, this feeling, he knew from other times as prison. Not where you were the prisoner, no, but where you were the walls.

The beam of a flashlight tracered across his face.

Rawbone looked up. Jack B approached while Doctor Stallings remained at the far end of the flatcar. "The kid with you. I heard he's sick bad."

Rawbone pointed his cigarette. The light swung toward the passenger car silhouetting that shawl-covered window.

"We don't pay slackers."

Rawbone did not look at Jack B. Instead he busied himself investigating the tip of his burning cigarette.

"Next stop, we're tossing him."

Rawbone smoked, then said, "Promise."

The light moved in on his face till it was more than a trifle too close. Still, there was no acknowledgment and the standoff was broken only by the warning cry of a train whistle well up the tracks.

TWENTY-FOUR

THERE CAME A second, longer warning call and the men began to lean out the car windows and crane their necks or stand at the edge of the flatcars, looking to where the trackline reached well into the black. Even in the women's car faces were hard-angled against the glass that steamed with their breath. The fleeting whistle soon fell away and there was only the sound of the Mastodon moving into that vast and murky landscape.

A guard on the tender shouted for Doctor Stallings and pointed a carbine as direction. Far off into the dead of night there appeared a pyre of flame. Singular and wind-taken. Doctor Stallings ordered the men to weapon up. He told Rawbone to remain on guard at the truck.

It took another quarter hour moving through the desert before they came upon a burning water depot and junction station for the Mexican Telegraph Company. A half-dozen slotted wood structures stood out in the dark like incinerated cages. The water tower had collapsed and was a smoldering ruin. The first train stood beyond the destruction. Guards from the coal car formed a protective perimeter. The second train stopped well short of the fires. Doctor Stallings and his officers moved in quick order upon the scene. The man in command of the first train waited on the tracks to report to Doctor Stallings. Rawbone leapt from the flatcar and came up the line enough to hear what was being said.

The fire was no mean accident of nature nor the foolish result of a human mistake, for there was no person nor animal, no vehicle nor wagon anywhere to be found. The man talking to Doctor Stallings pointed to a cross near three feet high made of wood slats that had been set in the sand beside the tracks. A printed sheet had been staked to it. It was a copy of a decree by the president pro tem Madero, from exile—the revolution had officially begun.

Mr. Stars and Stripes read the sheet after Doctor Stallings passed it to him and, when finished, slapped that paper with the back of his hand and said, "We got ourselves the war, commander."

The man in charge of the first train went over and pulled the cross out of the ground. He started back toward Doctor Stallings and was in the process of breaking it apart when there was a volley of rifle fire. Three, maybe four shots. Arterials of powdered cloth and blood jumped from his body and he was blown back onto the tracks still holding that crucifix, where he lay stretched out dead.

A firefight began. Flashbursts along the ravined darkness. Jack B led a group of guards to meet the attack under Stallings's command.

There was firing all up and down the line. Another man was hit and fell facedown in the sand. From the passenger car women screamed. Rawbone yelled for them to quiet and he knelt on one leg, rifle poised and ready.

He could hear the cries of horses as half a dozen riders spurred their mounts and dashed past one of the burning sheds that yawed and flared with the wind. Their shadows rose up immense and branded against the flames, there one moment and then gone.

Campesinos—the people.

They were in the midst of a war now. A shooting war. The gratification of political causes, thought Rawbone. The common assassin in him had scorn for such things.

Doctor Stallings walked past him checking the line and said, "You were right about one thing."

Rawbone asked, "One?"

"Casualties."

Once alone, Rawbone cursed his luck.

RIFLE FIRE STIRRED him. Through a waterish dim John Lourdes saw bits of flaming ash rush past the windows like some wind-riven army of stars. He thought he was back on that plat in the Hueco Mountains until he heard men outside shouting and the train begin to move.

His eyes cleared enough to see women all about him in the quietude. A hand rested on his shoulder and his eyes lifted and there was the girl Teresa sitting on the floor with her back against the wall beside him. She had in her other hand his notebook and pencil.

Of anyone he asked in Spanish, "How did I get here?"

The old crone answered and he lifted his head slightly. She, too, sat nearby, overseeing a watercan with a leather strap being heated over a bed of candles in the bottom of a clay bowl.

It turned out she was a curandera, or healer, named Sister Alicia. She was preparing teas of cayenne and Peruvian Samento. These he was given to drink and later, under watchful eyes, he slept.

With morning the trains entered the shipping yards of Chihuahua. A fog immersed the city. It clung to the earth and the trains made their slow and cumbersome way from switch to switch through a gray and otherworldly brew that floated about the wheels.

On the wall of a three-story brick warehouse someone had painted a vast but clumsy headstone with the name MALO on it. Standing at the edge of the flatcar urinating into that vapory murk Rawbone noticed, as he hitched his pants, Doctor Stallings atop the last passenger car surveying the yard. Both men were regarding the headstone. Rawbone used his derby as a pointer. "Not a chance, that happens!" he yelled.

He was sure Doctor Stallings spoke Spanish and knew the word malo meant "evil."

The train ferried past the roundhouse and the tooling sheds when came the sounds of cheering and gunfire. Figures began to appear out of the nothingness. Campesinos alive to the belief God was finally going to shine down his alien grace upon their lives, even if such grace were to be delivered by a little bloodshed.

They were everywhere in the mist. Rawbone could see them across the trainyard, hordes up on boxcars and clinging to the stacks of black and silent locomotives. They yelled to the men on the train and the women in the passenger cars, possessed as they were with the furious excitement of possibility.

One of the campesinos ran up to the flatcar and shouted that la revolución had begun and Rawbone answered with glorious indifference, smiling, "Yes, my friend, you've got a great future . . . behind you."

A woman now called to Rawbone from the landing of the passenger car. The young man, it seemed, was asking for him.

John Lourdes was pale and in pain, but the shivering had subsided and his mind steadied.

"I see the witches haven't killed you yet."

"Last night," he asked, "what happened?"

The father squatted. All around them were women watching. "War, Mr. Lourdes, that's what happened. We're right in the middle of a country that's goin' down for the count."

Sister Alicia was preparing another batch of medicinals. She poked Rawbone and told him to pass the cup to the young man. He took the steaming tin gingerly and ran it under his nose. The smell seemed to touch a nerve. Tangible it was with memories. He was torn by the moment then put it aside. "You got your magic down, don't you, you damn witch." He had a swallow himself. "Tastes of my youth," he said.

He passed the cup to John Lourdes, who sipped as he was told, "It seems our employer has a dog in this fight. I heard Mr. Stars and Stripes talking. Of course, I'm passing the information on to you as befitting our station."

The son thought on this a while. "But who is our employer? Mr. Hecht? Do you think so? I don't."

"I see your point, Mr. Lourdes."

The father stood. "Listen to me, you damn witches. Take care of the young master here. He's a true verdadero hombre." Rawbone grabbed his crotch. "Mucho caliente."

The women either laughed with embarrassment or turned away in disgust. "He's also a climber, in case you didn't know. Intends to make a name for himself. Thinks he can carry the weight of the world on his shoulders." He looked at Teresa, who was staring up at him. "You're in for a surprise."

As he started out, the son called to him. He wanted to say something but hesitated. He set the cup down, he brushed the hair back from his drawn face. "For bringing me in here . . . thank you."

To see him in such discomfort at having to say the thing gave Rawbone unequalled pleasure. Yet, to his absolute dismay, John Lourdes sounded utterly genuine.

TWENTY-FIVE

THEY EXISTED NOW in a state of war and so guards were stationed on the car roofs. Through a country that changed from lush canyons and fertile cropland to hills of boned and caking pumice, there was only that island of a train infinitesimal in a landscape marked by the eternal. Came nightfall they entered the Sierras, its remote and silent peaks rising toward a rind of moon. The tide of John Lourdes's bleeding had been stemmed and his reservoirs of strength were beginning to return.

He had asked the girl Teresa how she came to be on the train. She wrote that after her return from Immigration, her father grew more troubled and wary over her being picked up off the street. Even being brought home by the nuns as planned did nothing to ease his suspicions, so he arranged for her to be sent to the oil fields to work with these other women. He had brought her to the depot, then left with a handful of other men for Texas. She had anticipated his return, but she believed now something had befallen him.

John Lourdes confronted having to tell her the truth. He had near forced this moment from his first question. He asked her to join him on the back landing of the railroad car, and so she did. The church spire mountains all about them were run with spare pines. They could have been any young man and any young woman as they sat there looking out upon the blue majesty of evening. He lit a cigarette and wished it were so, but it was not.

To lie through silence was his first inclination. The why of it being he wanted the girl to think well of him, to be accessible to him, and keeping silent fed into his natural tendency toward dispassion.

But fever, exhaustion and pain diminished his defenses. As he lay in that car, watched over by those women, an action or turn of phrase, the way one laughed or prayed, all became fragments of the person that had once been his mother. And the closer he got to feelings of his mother, the more her presence filled him, the more intensely aware he became of the threatening musculature that was the father living inside him.

The man on the flatcar with the derby and that Savage .32 was the one who'd asked all those years ago in that open-air market in Juárez, "Do you want to know what people are really like, so you can never be tricked or fooled? Be indifferent to every man. Then you'll know."

Wasn't dispassion a possible disguise for indifference, the kind of indifference the father taught him? Lying in that train car he asked himself over and over: As there were fragments of his mother in those women, were there not fragments of the father in himself? Had he been poisoned as effectively as those customs guards at the ferry in ways he didn't realize?

This was what drove him to tell the girl the truth and so he wrote: *Your father was killed in the Hueco Mountains where he tried to murder two men.*

She read this and her eyes blinked. She absorbed the knowledge in painful increments. To see sadness in such composed quiet. She looked down at her folded hands. Her hair fell long across her face. Her beauty was her simple humanness. She gazed out into the night a long time. She was melancholy somewhere in the high mountains that were home to the wolves and the heavens.

She then looked at him with apprehension and foreboding. John Lourdes felt that look would go on forever, but, even so, he set pencil to paper. As he began to write what he had done, her hand came down and stopped him. Her action and her look spoke for themselves, for now she stood and went back into the car and he was left to the night.

"YOU KNOW WHAT a barrel of oil sells for today? Any idea? About fifty cents. Any idea what a war will do to that price?"

Jack B was holding court by the truck with a handful of branded felons and roustabouts while Rawbone sat behind the wheel and out of the sun. With his legs stretched up on the dash and arms folded, he let Mr. Stars and Stripes pontificate to see what information might come of it that he could pass on to Mr. Lourdes.

"Doctor Stallings says we could see prices reach a dollar . . . a dollar fifty a barrel by 1911. Oil stocks, that's what he's got his money in. Standard . . . American Eagle . . . Waters-Price. That's where his money is going and that's where," he slapped at the wallet hidden away in his back pocket.

"Mexico. You want to see what the future's going to look like, look no further than right here. You want to see a model for how the world will operate, look no further than right here. That's what Doctor Stallings tells me. And—"

"Right here and right now?" said Rawbone. He leaned up out of the seat and hooded his eyes with a hand and looked out over a passing landscape of brutal and barren contours that seemed to have no end.

"So this is the future. Well, if you don't mind, it looks a lot like hell if you ask me."

This brought out a few laughs and Jack B answered with, "You'll not only die ignorant, you'll die broke."

Rawbone sat back down in the cab and began to croon in his cracked and sandy voice, "Take me out to the ball game, take me out to the park . . ." He even got a few of the scurrilous guards to join in, which gave Jack B a good grinding. "Let me root, root, root for the home team, if they don't win it's a shame . . ."

He took the ridicule with a strained stare and then, looking beyond Rawbone, said, "Well."

It seemed John Lourdes had quietly made his way up the passenger side of the truck and now stood by the cab.

"How was your vacation?" asked Jack B.

The son glanced at the father. "Telling."

"I don't know if you heard. But Jack B here was just educating us on the future. Of course, I know your view of the future, Mr. Lourdes. There isn't one. There's just you, me and . . . American Parthenon, here."

"I heard Jack," said John Lourdes. He checked through his satchel on the cab floor and found an open and beat-up pack of cigarettes. He lit one and blew smoke out his nose in thin straight lines. "I think he makes a lot of sense."

Jack B turned his attention to Rawbone. "At least he won't die ignorant and broke."

"How do his employers measure it?" said John Lourdes.

"Employers?"

"Someone put this parade together," said Rawbone.

"Doctor Stallings. He's been the one commissioned."

"But someone had to checkbook all this up," said John Lourdes.

"I'm told he's got investors."

"Ah," said the son, looking toward the father, "investors."

"What was his sales pitch?" asked the father. He then winked with great pleasure at that group around the truck. "A dark alley and a loaded gun?"

"You'll die ignorant and broke," Jack B prophesied again as he walked off.

"But not soon."

It wasn't long after that gathering broke off into their own private schemes, leaving father and son alone.

"Well, Mr. Lourdes, what did you hear?"

"Someone else's version of the practical application of strategy."

"Aye. You know what I heard. Cuba . . . Manila . . . I've lived it. It's called military intervention. It's those bastards back at the Customs House. That's why all the Yankee Doodles at Fort Bliss. This is a shell game, Mr. Lourdes."

Silently the son assessed and reflected and then agreed. He continued to think and once or twice the father caught him looking back at the passenger car.

"Did you tell her?"

When he'd left, she was sitting on the floor of the passenger car in a profound sadness and could not, or would not, look at him. He went to Sister Alicia to thank her. He called her abuelita, which meant "grandmother," and told her she would never find him wanting if a time came and she were in need.

"I told her," said John Lourdes.

"Mr. Lourdes, in matters such as these, it is best to remain . . . indifferent."

THE FOLLOWING DAY they came upon the first train stopped in the white noon of sand hills. Three campesinos were being held at gunpoint by the guards. Two were young men, the third still a boy. Doctor

Stallings and his command officers went from the train and were informed these three had been caught trying to sabotage the tracks. The captured, of course, swore to their innocence.

Along the line of the second train the guards came out from the cars or took up on the landings and roofs to watch. Even the women stood in the sun with their heads covered and eyes hooded, to see. Only Rawbone showed no interest and remained in the truck cab with his legs up on the dash.

After much condemnation and many denials Doctor Stallings issued a series of quick orders. The three were marched to a bare and blackened tree surrounded by ocotillo that stood on a slope near fifty yards from the track. A rope was brought and Jack B flung it over what looked to be the sturdiest, though partly broken-off, branch. Doctor Stallings called to Tuerto.

"It's pictures you want."

He nodded, of course.

"It's pictures you'll have."

John Lourdes watched from the forward edge of the flatcar and from time to time he glanced back at the women. The girl Teresa alone had not come forward.

Doctor Stallings proceeded back up the slope followed by the photographer. John Lourdes noted how he went about the business at hand with mechanical clarity. He walked with his hands behind his back in a calm and studious manner, never raising his voice. It surprised John Lourdes when he thought how similar in methodology the Doctor was to Justice Knox.

The two older campesinos were ordered to their knees and when they refused Doctor Stallings nodded. Jack B quickly stepped behind both men and a single halo of powder exploded around their heads as a bullet was put into each of their brains. They lay side by side as if they intended to crawl away and the hot sand crackled where their blood threaded and then pooled.

The women were aghast and banded together, while some turned away in disgust. But this was not the last, nor the worst.

The boy had rushed to his compadres but was grabbed by the guards. He was then ordered taken to the tree. He fought the rope circling his neck like something crazed, but a force of pure strength proved too much and they had him leashed and lifted before he could even let out a cry.

The men stood back, for the boy kicked and spun. As his hands were not tied he took hold of the rope above his head and tried to lift himself to keep from strangling as he kicked out with his legs hoping to swing them around the trunk or to reach a branch and somehow save himself from a horrid death. His shoes were nothing more than strips of tire rubber cut and lashed around his feet and ankles and they scored the rotted bark in unending desperation.

It was an Inquisitional scene of madness, with the guards like statues upon a salted plain and the photographer Tuerto framing up this nightmare of a twisting soul. The women now were overwhelmed with crying and pleading to let the boy go or allow him to quickly die. It was the crone, Sister Alicia, who came forward then up that slope in a dress like that of a nun's habit in slow and faulted steps demanding they let the boy down, or end his suffering.

The climb for the old woman was hard and soon a figure was tramping through the sand behind her. It was the girl Teresa who came and took hold of Sister Alicia's arm and John Lourdes saw in her face the same elusive quiet and intense watchfulness as he had that first day by the fumigation shed.

Sister Alicia and the girl were met by a wall of straight-brimmed and squared-up men with stares like barren mountains. That aged witch meant to fight through them and though her paper flesh and frail bones failed her, that did not stop her fire to attempt an end. John Lourdes, watching the struggle, decided he had seen enough.

He leapt up onto the flatcar and as he did, far up the line, swaths of black registered upon the thermals. But for now he was set upon one course.

He reached into the cab for his rifle. The father went upright. "What are you doing, Mr. Lourdes?"

He hammered home a shell.

"Don't, Mr. Lourdes."

He turned and aimed. The sun burned his eyes, but he used the stillness of the men to strike a mark.

Rawbone promised damnation if he pulled the trigger.

John Lourdes heard, John Lourdes saw, and John Lourdes fired.

TWENTY-SIX

THE SUFFERING ENDED.

This was the first time the men around the tree reacted. They stared down toward John Lourdes as if they were a solemn jury. He turned from them. Far off in the cracked and barren hills they still hung there in the sky, planing above something as yet unknown—vultures.

"The country is having at you, Mr. Lourdes."

John Lourdes reached for the rifle scabbard in the truck cab.

"I remember a time back in the Huecos when you couldn't—"

"If you were wrung out, you wouldn't give up a drop of sympathy!"

"The road changes everyone," said the father in a manner that made the son want to put the rifle across his face.

"Even you," he said.

The father's eyes sparked.

"It's too bad it wasn't you they were hanging," said the son.

"You may get your wish." Rawbone motioned for John Lourdes to look around.

Jack B had gotten to the flatcar ahead of Doctor Stallings and the rest who were descending upon him. He demanded John Lourdes come down and confront him.

John Lourdes paid him no regard and stood where he was watching instead the curandera and the girl slowly hike past. Sister Alicia nodded to him a thank-you and then she and the others took to the passenger car.

Now he turned his attention to Jack B, who was still threatening him. By then Doctor Stallings was a few paces behind and John Lourdes said, "Doctor Stallings, before I go down there and boot this bastard, you better take a look to the southeast."

When he stared toward those capes of rock and squinted, he understood. With an economy of purpose Doctor Stallings ordered up a map, a signal pistol, flares, and two mounts taken from the boxcar to be saddled and ready in five minutes. He then ordered his men to their stations. Jack B was still staring up at John Lourdes asking, "You've had your say, now are you coming down?"

Doctor Stallings took his officer by the arm and ordered him to prepare the train and he asserted this command in no uncertain terms. As much as Jack B offered himself up as some sort of barbarian, he obeyed without argument or rancor. He obeyed Doctor Stallings not because of the weight and privilege of his position, but because of that other power that comes from the relentless pursuit of impunity.

John Lourdes and Rawbone were ordered from the train. When both had complied Doctor Stallings spoke first to John Lourdes. "Explain what you did."

"If you mean to kill something, do it on the first shot."

John Lourdes faced an unrelenting stare. "Pointed advice . . . that may well point also in your own direction."

"Understood," said John Lourdes.

Attention was then turned to Rawbone. "You hustled Mr. Hecht. And you didn't get the truck the way you claim you did."

"That's the bureaucrat in you talking."

"You're the type that lies even when the truth sounds better."

"Now, that's the professor in you talking?"

"I'm not challenging you over this. The truck is here. And, yes . . . there are casualties. And there'll be more."

He pointed at the two horses just yards away and near saddled. "You notice there are two horses." The map was brought to him, as were the signal pistol and flares. He set them on the flatcar.

He stood very close to Rawbone, who leaned against the flatcar. "I was a professor, as you seem to know, at some of the finest colleges in America. Teaching is what I would call an unchallenging pastime. Nothing ultimately critical happens in a classroom. The setting lacks grandeur and, more important, finality."

He reached out and took the Savage automatic from Rawbone's belt. He looked the weapon over carefully, handling it with a professional's interest. "There is a book, and you could have walked right out of its pages. It is about murder. There is a devil and a Grand Inquisitor. And there is one idea in the book that repeats itself. An idea that would appeal to you as it does to me . . . 'All things are lawful.'"

Doctor Stallings replaced the weapon in Rawbone's belt.

Rawbone then reached out and brushed away bits of sand from the shoulder of the commander's gray suit coat. "The story doesn't exactly spark of Horatio Alger, does it?"

The mounts were brought over. Doctor Stallings handed the signal gun and bandoleer of flares to John Lourdes. "You both will earn your money today," he said, spreading the map on the flatbed floor.

THE FATHER AND son proceeded from the train with the sun hard against their shoulders, watched by the commander and his company of guards. Even the girl Teresa, from window after window, followed the slow climb of their mounts upon an eroded hill face.

From the map it seemed the vultures marked a military garrison, sited to protect a junction where the lines divorced into parallel tracks, both running to Tampico and the oil fields.

"The doctor knows how to frame a warning," said the son.

"You thought his little speech a warning. I hoped it was a compliment, or at least an insult."

"He didn't have the authority for what he did, no matter. He even ordered a picture, no matter."

"Who did El Presidente have build those tracks? Who financed them? America and the Brits. They own the rails like they own the oil fields. That gives him the authority. And the Mexican, he's heir to the fuckin' sand."

They heard the heavy breathing of a mount and the chinging of bridle metal and came about to see Tuerto chugging a mule forward to try and catch up.

"Where are you going?" asked John Lourdes.

Tuerto pointed to the vultures.

"On whose authority?"

He held up his camera.

"Another fuckin' genius," said the father.

Through a dry and sweeping wind the mule followed in the horses' tracks. Rawbone spoke out to the world around him, "Three wise men tramping to Bethlehem."

The garrison was a quadrangle of mud buildings connected by a palisade of sharpened stakes where sat an army of hunched and drowsy-faced vultures. A loosely roped gate hung slightly open. They dismounted and John Lourdes fired his shotgun into the air. The

162

creatures flushed skyward and hung momentarily on the dead air and then descended to the rooftops.

The men went forward and Rawbone pushed the gate with his rifle and before them opened a small amphitheatre of death. They covered their noses and mouths with bandanas. They entered the compound. Flies everywhere, and the stench. A dozen soldiers bloating in the sun. The buildings had been ransacked and personal possessions lay strewn about the enclosure.

John Lourdes saw a stairwell that led up to a rooftop watchtower. He took binoculars from around his neck and as he ascended vultures retreated from the vigas, their steps like drunken old men. Under an overhang the father saw a table and on it was a Victrola. He looked at the pile of records beside it. One read Brahms' Lullaby. He set the record on the turntable and cranked up the player. A Spanish version began.

Music drifted out over that dusty pueblo and into the desert beyond. John Lourdes had been studying the country and the trackline and pulled the binoculars from his eyes and looked down into the enclosure. Tuerto walked amongst the dead taking photographs. And the father—he had found a chair and was sitting in the shade by the Victrola, the bandana shielding his nose and mouth, the rifle across his lap and that haunting child's melody—he could well have been the Lord of some Breugheled damnata.

This, thought the son, is what I was born from. Can this be the man who in his youth touched my mother's heart on a trolley in the Texas rain? Can this be the man who even for bare moments breathed love? John Lourdes wondered, if God truly put a soul in each living being, could it be the soul was capable of flaming out so completely it no longer existed, so all that was left was a living husk as horrible as the enclosure where they stood?

Yet, he was not as waylaid as he felt he should have been looking down upon this wretched scene. Did it mean that in some way his own soul was burning down to become a useless cinder that would knock around inside his chest wherever he walked upon the earth? Or was this some rite of passage the part of him that was the father came to prepare him for? The father's words worked like cruel and busy claws inside him: "This country is having at you, Mr. Lourdes . . . the road changes everyone."

Then from behind the bandana came that crackly voice. "I see you there, Mr. Lourdes . . . looking down on me."

"You better get up here," said the son.

John Lourdes sat on the roof wall writing in his notebook, and when the father joined him the vultures again flared and fell away. The son pointed his pencil at the binoculars set on the adobe ledge. "Tell me what you see."

The father took the binoculars and panned over that whinstone prairie. The land trembled with heat but there was nothing save where the track turned out to become separate rail lines that looked to be near burned into the earth.

"I see unadulterated nothing."

John Lourdes finished writing. He yelled for Tuerto. He tore the page from his notebook and stood. "One of the tracks has been sabotaged."

The father's head arched back and the son turned him about. He stood behind him with an arm leaned over his shoulder. He was as close now as the father had been to the son that night in the Hueco Mountains, only now it was the son's shouldered weapon that insinuated itself.

"With the binoculars . . . about fifty yards up from the turnout. To the left. Laying off in the sand away from the tracks. You'll see it."

And so he did. It looked to be embossed in the sand. A long bulky strip of metal. Smooth as could be.

"What the hell is it?"

"It's a fishplate . . . It's what they use to bolt the rails together. You can see it's been removed from one of the tracks. So has another one at the other end of the rail and you can see . . . the spikes are missing. That rail is just sitting on the ties waiting for a train."

TWENTY-SEVEN

TUERTO AGREED TO carry John Lourdes's note back to the train. Doctor Stallings reviewed it with his officers and proceeded accordingly. The plan was to bring the trains on to the garrison, then wait for John Lourdes to signal. Son and father were to scout the secondary trackline to Tampico, spotting up the rails for further sabotage. Doctor Stallings walked the turnout and the engineer showed him where the fishplates and spikes had been removed. Doctor Stallings looked to his watch, to the south. He sat quietly on the locomotive steps waiting for John Lourdes to signal. In packs of two and three the guards asked Tuerto about the garrison that now stood in shadow on the hilltop. He would describe the scene and then point to the aperture of his camera and tell them it had all been captured there and prints could be had for a commission. Even the women, appalled by what they heard, clung to every whisper for the dead belonged to the government and that aroused unspoken hopes.

From a craggy plateau John Lourdes and Rawbone scouted the hills before them. A hundred miles beyond, the Gulf washed up on the beaches of Tampico.

"You can smell the salt air from here," said the father. Then bringing his horse about, called out, "Mr. Lourdes." He pointed. To the west of the train, tracers of dust were piling up across the benchland.

John Lourdes got out his binoculars. "It's not dragoons. And they're coming on like religion."

"They're going to hit the train."

The bandoleer of flares was slung over John Lourdes's neck. He shoved the binoculars back in his saddlebags. He got out the signal gun. The father rode up alongside him.

"Before you warn them. You know what I'm going to say. Tampico . . . the oil fields. You don't need them back there. If they make it, well . . . and the women are not your province. Tampico . . . the oil fields."

John Lourdes loaded a flare.

"You can fill notebooks till you fall over dead but what you need to write . . . Justice Knox shouldn't have entrusted you with this. You're not the right man for it." His eyes were black and hard, the neck cords strained. "You wanted to get there, we can get there. It ends when you say it ends, right. There it is out there. The practical application of strategy means you stay indifferent and take advantage when advantage can be taken. Isn't that why you ended up here, why I ended up here? Answer me, Goddamn it."

ONE FLARE SIGNALED all was clear, two flares there was trouble and hold back. To that John Lourdes added a third option in his note. Three flares meant trouble, but come on quick. When Doctor Stallings, standing atop the tender, raised three fingers, Jack B ordered the trains out and weapons readied.

From the plateau John Lourdes could see banners of gray smoke against the haze and he knew the trains were on the move.

"You . . . me . . . and the truck!" shouted the father. "Alright . . . I hope the BOI taught you how to board a moving train under fire."

The trains went through a gap in the hills. Small islands of dust with riders at the fore descended scrub ridges and rose up magically out of distant swales. Rurales with bandoleers crisscrossing their chests like ancient baldrics and filthy hats and straw sombreros, and they carried carbines and flintlocks and five-shot Colts and machetes and bows and arrows and their saddlebags and stirrups winged outward and the fronds of their hats bent back as they drove to flank the trains.

There were bursts of rifle smoke along the length of the cars and riders crumpled out of their saddles and horses crushed down upon their hooves and flipped over brokenly. Against a barren sky John Lourdes scanned that tableland with binoculars to see how and where fate might intervene for them to get back on the train.

As the lead train cleared a long shelf of battened stone, a mass of trampling shadows surged from hiding. The men in the coal car out front of the locomotive leaned up from their parapets and poured fire down into the clustered features of men close enough to touch.

A rurale with a leather breastplate and hair to his shoulders whipped his horse up alongside the rails and was cut down as he flung a stick of dynamite. It disappeared within the black hull and caromed off the casement with fuse hissing. Men scrambled to reach it but were too late.

The explosion rocked the coal car. Men were thrown over the rim. The black wheels lifted, then slammed down, missing the rails. The wheels sawed ties and scored earth and the plough-shaped pilot rammed the coal car housing and all that tonnage lifted and scythed across the engine tearing the stack and the menagerie of steel and steam was engulfed in smoke. A part of the frame housing tore across the connecting rods and they broke loose from the locomotive spearing the boiler and a gauge wheel in the cab blew into the chest of the engineer and drove his ribs right out through his back.

The locomotive surged and the coal car listed into a decline beside the tracks, only to be vaulted up again where it broadsided the engine. For a few moments this architecture of ruined metal and mangled steel plowed on at full speed and then the housing plates separated at the seams and there was a violent hiss and a rush of flame and the remains of train cars exploded into a volcano of dust and debris.

John Lourdes swept from the plateau and down a ravine with Rawbone in hard pursuit. Their horses struggled up a steep incline from where they could see through the settling smoke that the first train was a hissing mass strewn over the tracks.

The second train was a mile back and coming on fast. It was under heavy fire from a cavalry of poor wretches hunkered down in their saddles and firing over the outstretched heads of their mounts.

John Lourdes wiped the sweat and dust from his field glasses and surveyed the landscape again. If the train could get past the wreckage, he saw where the tracks traversed a rising battlement of hills and the train would have to slow drastically. He yelled to Rawbone and pointed to where they were to ride. The father shouted back, as his mount shouldered wildly, that the train would never get through. But the son had already spurred his horse toward where the walls of the canyon burned with daylight.

They came up out of a ravine. The ground before them was clouded with dust. They dashed past a howling band of outriders making for the train. They were in the midst of gunfire now, charging toward a shaly ridge with their weapons drawn. A pack of rurales swept off after them in pursuit. One of their mounts was shot from under him and the man was flung to the earth and his own compadres trampled over him with stunning disregard.

Rawbone had not come unprepared and he took from his shirt a grenade and flung it back at their pursuers. A rain of metal shards ended the pursuit. Men and mounts were torn asunder with ruthless efficiency. Belts of flesh and leather marked the earth where they once had been.

The great Mastodon thundered toward the smoking gauntlet that littered the tracks. Doctor Stallings stood in the locomotive with the engineer while Jack B was atop the tender hunched down as he fired and fielded orders. There were men in the cars trying to hold back the blood from their seeping wounds. There were men dead. There were riderless mounts with their wild manes charging alongside burning rail-cars. The dust and smoke from this nightmare frieze rose up out of the earth for miles.

The engineer looked to Doctor Stallings. "She won't get through," he said.

"Throttle it," came the order.

"We'll wreck."

"Throttle it."

"We'll wreck."

"Then we'll wreck."

The engineer did as he was ordered. They could feel the pure force of the speed as the huge wheels began to reverb against the rails. The hammering of the pistons driving steam through the valves grew to near deafening.

A horseman with a bow and arrow rode upon the locomotive's shadow. Tethered to the shaft was a lit stick of dynamite. Doctor Stallings turned and fired. The horseman was taken from the saddle just as the arrow left the bowstring. It rattled between the engine and the tender and exploded just beyond. The first car shook, windows shattered, men were thrown to the floor.

The distance between the train and those scorched and battered remains that formed a breastwork along the rails closed with fiendish speed. Doctor Stallings heard the engineer asking the Almighty to remember him in heaven seconds before hell arrived on impact.

Across that barren pan, above the rifle fire and the shouting and cries of the wounded, were the crushing grate and shrill of steel on steel unlike anything the mind could conjure sending a shock wave down the length of the couplings such that the women in the last car were flung over and atop each other.

Son and father reached the mouth of the canyon and were leading their mounts on foot up a screed hill face that looked down on the tracks. Like some foundried Atlas the Mastodon shouldered the brunt of the wreckage. The huge steamer rocked and shunted and slowed and the wheels locked and lost traction and were skidding uselessly. But when the wheels caught and the valves opened, driving the rods forward, the savaged hull of that coal car got screeched from the tracks—the train was through.

The engineer was pale and shaken. He looked to Doctor Stallings and nodded and Doctor Stallings leaned past him and pulled the train whistle. Across the plain a call of defiance.

The train was minutes from the ledge where John Lourdes leaned over and looked down at the tracks.

"We'll jump from here," he said.

Rawbone was behind him and glanced at the rails and saw if things went bad it was a chasm and the rocks and an inauspicious end.

"Mr. Lourdes," he said, "China looks closer."

The train passed through a cut in the rock. Jack B stood on the tender firing down at the last cadre of riders whose mounts had not failed them or fallen back in exhaustion. The train was close enough now John Lourdes could make out the flag inked into the muscles of that shooting arm.

The ground dropped and rose with outcroppings of rock, and the riders drove their mounts over this tortured masonry to the point of death. As the train pulled away one rurale on a raw and maneless beast got off an arrow before the forelegs buckled and the withers fell.

The arrow lifted and turned as John Lourdes leapt to a passenger car roof. It descended, picking up speed in a long whoosh as Rawbone followed suit, cursing the world all the way back to creation but making sure the one thing he didn't lose was his derby. The arrow embedded in the deckboards of a flatcar. The fuse to the dynamite lashed to the shaft hissed and sparkled as both men jumped the couplings from car to car where guards lay dead as the train hiked it up through that causeway along the rimrock.

They stood beside the truck exhausted. Dust streaked where it had caked to the sweat running down their faces and for a few moments they were neither son and father nor federal agent and common assassin, but two men swept up in the machinery of wholesale slaughter who had momentarily escaped with their lives.

The father put the barrel of his rifle to the barrel of the son's as if to acknowledge their surviving. Just then the spark of the fuse along the shaft of the arrow bottlenecked with all that packed graphite and blew the deck of the flatbed in front of them to pieces.

TWENTY-EIGHT

THE PURE FORCE of the concussion lifted John Lourdes onto the truck hood. Rawbone was tumbled down the length of the flatcar only to come up on his knees gritting his teeth in pain. A spike of bracing protruded from the back of his shoulder blade.

He knelt on the deck trying to reach around and pull it out, but he couldn't get a hold and it was left to John Lourdes, clearing his head and staggering over, to jimmy the stake loose while the father growled and cursed the vile thing out.

Standing, he said to the son, "Mr. Lourdes, for a moment I thought it was you putting a shiv to me."

"Yeah, seeing you on your knees . . . I thought you took up religion."

The flatcar ahead of them, from its screw block to end beam, was pure wreckage. Part of the deck smoldered, part burned. Guards rushed from the cars ahead to blanket the flames. John Lourdes pulled a tarp from the truck to attack the fire and the father, with blood seeping down the back of his shirt, moved to help him when came a terrible jolt that froze both men. What followed was the deck beneath them as it hitched and sidled.

The father was confused, but John Lourdes, with absolute and unequivocal knowledge, understood what this meant. He dropped the tarp, rushed to the edge of the flatcar and, kneeling, looked over the buffer. The coupler of the flatcar ahead had been torn from its screw block. It hung there, attached to the coupler of their flatcar like the dead claw of some iron monster.

John Lourdes stood.

"Mr. Lourdes?"

"We've been cut loose."

The train cars were moving forward through a sweeping passway toward the ridgeline, but it took only a few moments for their section to slow and the one ahead to pull away. The guards trying to tamp down the flames stopped and just stared dumbly.

John Lourdes knelt again and leaned out over the end beam, craning his neck to check the undercarriage.

The father, in pain and bleeding, called to him and John Lourdes steadied back up, his face strained. He stared down into that decline of hills from whence the train had come, trying to calculate how far—at least a mile he thought—before that first turn up from the desert floor where the track was cut through the rock face.

"Mr. Lourdes?"

"The air brakes should hold . . . if they haven't been damaged. But if they have—"

The women were on the landing and called out trying to understand. The father came up slowly, favoring his wound, so the son lent him a hoist. The train reached the sun line and soon there was only the faint trailing of its engine smoke.

"They'll come back."

John Lourdes was waiting, feeling, listening—would the brakes hold? "You know what it takes to stop a train on the downgrade? It's like keeping back an avalanche. And reversing it back uphill . . ."

"They'll not leave the munitions."

"Neither will we. Get the women up here and off this train, but ahead of it."

John Lourdes crossed to the passenger car landing and pushed past the women and their questions and ran on through the car as the father cursed out orders for them to get over and be quick. Rawbone helped them with a hand or caught them when they jumped and he herded them to the front of the flatbed while he damned their womanly souls.

John Lourdes surveyed the bracings under the back landing and knew there were extra chains on the flatcar for the maneuver he had in mind. When he turned, he saw Teresa standing off alone watching him. But the wary eyes and the collected silence were now clouded with fear and confusion. He went to her and as he put out a hand, his boots had the first hint the cars were slipping backward. The air brakes were failing.

The last of the women jumped from the train and crowded up on the tracks. John Lourdes brought Teresa and, with Rawbone, lifted her down from the flatcar. The train was inching backward and stopping the car became imperative before it picked up speed. By the side railings were piles of heavy chain. John Lourdes dragged one loose and hoisted it up on his shoulder, then ordered Rawbone to bring another as the brakes were giving way.

John Lourdes was at the rear of the passenger car kicking off the door when Rawbone dumped a coil of chain at his feet.

"What are you trying?"

John Lourdes was gasping and his shirt soaked through. As he started to explain, the father went down on one knee and favored his scored shoulder.

The son intended to swing one chain through the door and out a landing window and noose it. He'd do the same on the other side of the door with the other landing window. Then they'd get enough chain and hook it to both nooses and drop it over the landing platform and onto the tracks and up under the wheels to form a kind of wedge braced to the car.

The father looked about and questioned, "Will it work?"

"I saw it done once, but not on an incline like—"

Framed in the far passenger door was Teresa. Most of a heavy chain was slung up on her shoulder and the rest dragged like a metal umbilicus. She was bent and straining torturously with each step.

"What in the name of madness," said the father.

She'd fashioned a reason to act, watching them haul the chains, and she'd climbed back up onto the flatcar with the women grabbing at legs and skirt to restrain her. She couldn't negotiate the door dragging all that iron and when the men reached her Rawbone took all that weight upon himself.

John Lourdes, with his palms facing down, patted at the air as his way of asking Teresa to hold where she was. Rawbone carried that iron monstrosity to the rear of the car. John Lourdes hooked each end of the chain to one of the nooses. Then he had the father help him loop it over the back platform and it landed on the tracks with an immense clang.

"When I give the order to cinch it, get inside fast and keep going. This platform may come off and part of the wall with it."

Each link was near as big as their fists and they scarred and danged along the rails as John Lourdes took a deep breath. The father muscled down like a prizefighter and then John Lourdes yelled out, "Cinch it."

They roped in the chain. It tautened and caught up against the wheels. The two men scrambled over each other getting into the car and the sound coming off those locked wheels was like a foundry saw shearing pure steel. There were fireworks of sparks, and the studs in the platform and up through the rear wall began to spider with cracks and the platform ripped apart like a flimsy toy. The back wall was there one moment, and the next, they were staring out a frame of decimated wood exposing drab brown hills and dust-strewn daylight. The screeching went on, it seemed, interminably. Then, in one staggering instant the cars stopped.

SECTIONS OF THE chain were ground to dust, but the remainder was shivved up under and around the wheels and so the cars were held.

The Mastodon had not returned and they were left now to their own resources in that silent chasm, with Tampico a century of miles through those fluted and waterless hills.

"Now," said John Lourdes to the father, "you see why I wouldn't leave the truck."

It was in its own way a purely orthodox application of practical strategy. The father still remarked with a certain insight, "That's not why you wouldn't leave the truck."

John Lourdes got out the fire ax and a set of crowbars and formed two work gangs of women. The father took the first bunch and they went about chopping the roof beams loose from the passenger car. The son worked the others dismantling the flatbed siderails and truss bars. And damn if that common assassin didn't start teaching those women to sing in English "Take Me Out to the Ball Game" as they sweated it in that filthy railcar.

John Lourdes meant to build a rampway jerry-rigged from an assemblage of crisscrossed timbers and truss bound together by rope and cable and parts of chain and any clothing the women weren't wearing right then and there.

John Lourdes walked up and down this raft with uncertainty as the father and the women watched.

"It's no masterpiece," said the son.

"Mr. Lourdes, good manners requires me to allow you first crack at driving the truck."

"You're a fuckin' saint," muttered the son under his breath.

John Lourdes edged the truck over the lip of the flatcar and leaned from the cab to see if the weight could be sustained. The father acted as traffic cop angling his hands to get those wheels a little this way or that. When the engine was committed all the way down the ramp it started to sag like the spine of some cartoon swayback. The women chimed in trying to avert what they saw as a disaster, yelling for John Lourdes to turn the wheels in direct contradiction to the father who was now cursing their hellish mouths. Some of them took to pleading he go back, while others urged he just come on. It was all devolving into useless jabber so John Lourdes swallowed hard to clear his throat and with one quick to-hell-with-it decision, gassed the pedal.

The truck lurched, and as the front end touched ground the ramp gave and the rear tires slammed upon the ties. The truck heaved to one side under the strain of those lashed crates of ammunition and all watched in stunned silence as the unwieldy hump piled up in the truckbed settled back in place. Then John Lourdes just footed the gas pedal slightly and the truck started forward to a collective sigh of relief.

TWENTY-NINE

BY DUSK THEY drove the trackline, one wheel straddling the ties and the other on a meager strip of roadbed. The women took turns perched up on crates, stacked in the truckbed or walking ahead of it. One man drove while the other rested. It was slow and dangerous and when they reached the peak at nightfall below them was the immense void of the desert floor.

The women proceeding ahead of the truck now took to carrying lanterns or candles to guide the way. The lights fireflied in that steep and treacherous canyon, where their shadows walked in slow and somber order like some druidic procession moving through the vast church of the night.

When it was Rawbone's time to turn the wheel over to John Lourdes, he took up with the others in the truckbed, sitting on boxes of hand grenades and machine-gun belts. And while Sister Alicia stitched the wound in his back with sewing thread, he led a chorus of singing women in their slanted English:

> Let me root, root, root for the home team
> If they don't win it's a shame
> For it's one, two, three strikes, you're out
> At the old ball game.

Later that night John Lourdes wrote in his notebook: *You helped the old woman and risked yourself . . . you carried the chains . . . you're sitting with me now . . .* He ended what he wrote with a question mark he circled.

He and Teresa sat in the truck together, wedged up amongst the crates as they crossed all that black and windy emptiness.

She read his questions and then wrote: *I helped Sister Alicia because she needed help and it was right . . . I carried chains because chains were necessary . . . I am sitting with you now because forgiveness is needed.*

He wrote: *I am thankful you can forgive me.*

She replied: *This is not just about you.*

She had not fully realized how much her father was of those men on the slope executing a child. And that her father was of the same blood and history as the dead turned her stomach.

She added to what she wrote: *I am small against this world . . . but the Christ inside my heart is greater yet. Without forgiveness all of life is forsaken. I will not become forsaken.*

John Lourdes could hear his own father's voice from behind the steering wheel. In the cab with him were Sister Alicia and another woman. He had them rehearsing lyrics to "Yankee Doodle Dandy."

He stared into his notebook. He absorbed what Teresa had written. He could feel her beside him. He knew without asking, the forgiveness extended to her own father. It was tangible as rain upon an upturned face. I am small against this world . . . These words, he knew, were true about himself, in that place, at that moment, though forgiveness was not an option.

THEY DROVE STRAIGHT into the dawn. Limestone chasms gave way to islands of scrub pine. The earth was sandy and the truck struggled mile after mile. The stones of the desert began to warm with the sun. To the north a pale outline on the horizon, a meager oasis of huts.

Near Tamuin they passed an abandoned cathedral upon the desert floor. Magnificent it was, from the era of the Conquistadors. Red were its stone walls and grand dome against a hot and cloudless sky. The women blessed themselves as they drove past, for with God there was no forgotten place.

They dined by a stream near a fallen hacienda. Amongst the trees a rusting iron fence enclosed a few headstones. Names the wind and sun had stolen. Rawbone watched John Lourdes and the girl Teresa walk along the shallows. The water was cool and shiny in the quieting light and the breeze gave the brush that soft and brittle song.

There was something about the long blue light of dusk that for Rawbone always felt of eventuality and of being forlorn. He looked at the fallen hacienda, then the small family of graves set amongst the trees. He put his cigarette out in the sand and stood as John Lourdes and the girl walked past. He tipped his hat to her gracefully.

"Mr. Lourdes," he said, "you better be careful." He smiled. "This is how people end up with their own little Cains and Abels."

THEY DROVE TOWARD the moonlight, and it was a woman atop the highest crates who first sighted Tampico and called to the others. Piercing the misty Gulf air a vast spangle of lights. A mile farther they came upon railroad tracks. Out of the smoky dark a lone freight approached with a great rattling of cars and the fierce call of its whistle. Tankers destined for the oil fields.

The day arrived damp and muggy. They were just a dozen miles from Tampico and had to stop to gas the truck with the last of the reservoir they carried in drums. The women were exhausted and filthy. As they stoked up a fire to make coffee and greased dough with sugar, the father asked the son to walk off a ways so they could talk privately.

"Mr. Lourdes, I buddied once with a top-floor felon. Part Sioux. It was right here in Tampico, after I came back from that joke of a war in Manila. He gave me advice once . . . 'Raw . . .' he called me, 'Raw . . .' he said, 'when things go bad, every road out of town is the black road.'"

He waited to see how John Lourdes would react. Measured silence was the answer.

"We got all that ammunition, Mr. Lourdes. I say we bury a wallet's worth, tell Stallings we lost it in transit. We'd have it to sell if we needed money. You'd have it to sell if you needed to buy or bribe information. Or if . . . we find ourselves on the black road."

John Lourdes took out a cigarette. He had no matches, so he put out a hand for the father to drop him one. He eyed Rawbone with a quizzing stare. After he got the cigarette lit John Lourdes asked, "What happened to this . . . top-floor felon?"

"He was shot to death in his sleep."

"I'd have bet on poisoning."

"Thank you, Mr. Lourdes. Professional compliments are always appreciated."

"Of course, at the end of this, with all your smile and good cheer, you discovered there wasn't quite the future down here you expected—"

"You might offer me those crates as a stipend for my outstanding service."

"I don't know when you're worse. When you're actually worse, or when you're not."

THEIR RIG LABORED along a shipping road that was deeply rutted from the rains and heat and heavily trafficked with oil trucks and supply wagons and laborers on foot. They were a sight with all those women stacked up on that stepped mountain of crates like some skirted aviary. Men called out from truck cabs or whistled and undressed the ladies with their eyes. As the road ascended it gave way to the Gulf and the world of Tampico and the oil fields spread out before them. Only this was not the vision as presented in the Díaz film John Lourdes had watched in the dark of the funeraria.

This was a hallucinatory contradiction. A fetid kingdom of pure commerce and profane destruction. A land stripped of life now cancered from fire and oil.

"El auge," said Rawbone.

The oil boom. The phrase encompassed everything but captured nothing.

Tampico had been established along the Panuco River, which flowed into the Gulf. The town was cordoned by a series of lagoons and marshes. There was a vast railroad yard, and the river had become an oil turnpike of tugs and barges, flatbeds and tankers, paddle wheelers; anything that could stay afloat and carry freight was on that waterway.

The rainforests had been cut down and burned off and now grimy wells rose up into the sky. By the Pueblo Viejo Lagoon was a place known as Tankerville, where row after row of wood and concrete drums, an armada of storage bins, baked in the sun. Neighborhoods had been constructed in the marshes, with shacks of cratewood and slat for workers built on stilts as the ground beneath oozed up slime. Swamps were drained for warehouses and pump stations and shipping terminals.

Everywhere they looked there were black pools of oil. Pits had been dug for spills. There were lakes where wells had blown and bled upon the earth for days that now were turning to a gloppy asphalt in the coastal heat. The high reeds along the lagoons were tipped with the black of oil, the trees were marked with it, the roads and roofs spotted with it, wagons, cars and trucks, their tires turned with it. The black rolled in with the tide and tainted the sand with it.

The air was dense and filmy and they could taste the work of the refineries on their tongues and the scent of its rancid perfume bitter to the nostrils.

The father glanced across the cab at the son, who was behind the wheel hunting for the Agua Negra offices. "Mr. Lourdes, the American and Brit companies have a billion dollars in this. They know what packets of money and a sense of purpose can do." He threw out his arm to take in all that they could see. "By their standards . . . I am just a common assassin."

They drove through the railyards. Hundreds of workers were being unloaded from freight cars and herded into lots like cattle or goats. El Enganche—the Hooking—was what the process was called. Peasants from farms and villages in the hills were recruited at bazaars and carnivals by wily agents known as enganchadors who promised transportation, free room and board and three to four pesos a day if the peasant contracted to work for a period of time. Of course, when they reached Tampico, they would be told by the companies that the contract was not to be honored and that pay amounted to one peso a day. More than they might ever make in some rural pisshole, but the cost of living in Tampico turned them into hard-working indigents.

The father tapped the dashboard with his knuckles to draw John Lourdes's attention to an array of wall graffiti defiling the Yankee and the Brit. It was not the first run of epithets seen chalked on a wall about the state of mind the people had toward the brutal realities in Tampico.

"The women up top," said the father, "are heading for the same fate as those bummers on the train."

John Lourdes knew this, though it was the first he'd ever actually contended with that fact. It was not something he should involve himself in, yet he stopped the truck and got out. He then began to explain to the women what their future held.

It was not news, he discovered. A girl not much older than Teresa summed up their response by holding out and opening a small but empty purse.

When John Lourdes started the truck back up the father asked, "Mr. Lourdes, would you say I'm an intelligent man?"

"Sadly . . . I would."

"You should have left the truck in the desert. You should have left the women at the train. You should not have done what you just did. You are driving straight toward ruin."

THIRTY

THE AGUA NEGRA offices were on the Fiscal Wharf. A dredger was docked beside a pile hammer punching at the river bottom. The wharf was crowded with traffic for the tankers. Jack B was out in front of the rolling doors of a two-story shed having a smoke when he spotted this flock of women riding atop a truck. He was a figure of astonishment when John Lourdes pulled up in front of him.

Rawbone tipped his hat. "Not even a hello?" He stepped out of the cab. "Would you be so kind as to tell the good doctor we've brought the truck."

Jack B disappeared inside the shed without so much as a word.

"There goes a starved mind," said the father.

John Lourdes now stepped out of the truck and the women climbed down from the back. It wasn't long before Doctor Stallings walked into the daylight followed by a handful of officers and guards. As Rawbone expected, Stallings was not felled with astonishment but rather maintained the deadpan mask that was his trademark.

He looked to John Lourdes. "Your note . . . it may well have made the difference for us."

Doctor Stallings ordered Jack B to get the women organized. He then asked John Lourdes how they managed the Sierras. He walked around the truck while John Lourdes explained. The father watched Doctor Stallings intently. When finished, as an afterthought, John Lourdes said, "We lost a few crates before we had the cars braked."

The doctor listened silently. He told Jack B to get the women to the field cafeteria. "Except this one and this one." He singled out Alicia and the girl Teresa.

He then ordered both men into the truck and joined them. As John Lourdes slipped behind the wheel, Teresa signaled him as if to say goodbye. Doctor Stallings directed them to drive up along the Panuco. He sat with arms folded and offered no conversation until he began to point out the tank farms that lined the river. The Aquilla . . . National Petroleum . . . Waters-Price . . . Standard Oil . . . East Coast Gulf . . . The Gulf Coast . . . The Huasteca . . . and those were only the northern fields.

"Gentlemen," he said, "this has become its own nation."

Amidst an array of boiler stacks and paraffin plants and refineries was a garrison of long, low huts and a corrugated warehouse. A sign posted above the gate read:

AGUA NEGRA
OIL FIELD SECURITY

The men there were of the same lot as those on the train and they drew up and became attentive when they recognized it was Doctor Stallings in the truck. They pulled up to the warehouse garage. Rawbone and John Lourdes followed Doctor Stallings to his office. It was Spartan: a desk, a half-dozen phones. Both men were asked for their security cards. When Doctor Stallings had them in hand, he tore them up.

"You no longer work for Agua Negra."

He waited for either man's response. Something seemed to pass between the father and son. An unspoken sense to remain silent. Doctor Stallings took petty cash from a drawer. He slid the stack of bills toward John Lourdes. "You're cut loose. Go to the Southern Hotel. Get a room where the both of you can bunk. Take the motorcycle. If anyone asks, you're not working for us."

John Lourdes took the money and pocketed it. He glanced at the father.

"He's staying," said Doctor Stallings.

When they were alone, Rawbone took out a cigarette and lit it. He removed his derby and set it on a wood filing cabinet. He went and sat in a chair by the window.

"Those oil fields," said Doctor Stallings, "they're not as big as Texas, but they stand to have a lot more influence. The companies here will be thought of as a country in the near future. And they are beginning to learn how to be one. The practicals and priorities."

Rawbone set a leg up on the chair and rested an arm on his knee. "You made a point of referencing Texas."

"Your legal situation."

"As Mr. Stars and Stripes is fond of saying . . . this ain't Texas."

"And that is the point."

They heard motorcycle gears shifting and an engine whine. Rawbone could see out the window and past the wire fencing John Lourdes taking to the road through burned and trampled weeds.

"Do you fully trust him?"

Rawbone laughed inwardly. "I fully trust myself."

"You will ultimately have to come to a decision about that. You'll be given the truck. You can hire out. Someone I know will contact people on your behalf. I'll tell them they can reach you at the Southern Hotel. You're an independent contractor now."

"To what end?"

There was not a blank in his thoughts, nor a gap in the response. "An assassination," he said.

Rawbone walked out into the fucking light with the foretaste of death thick in his mouth. He knew, now, with an absolute clarity that Doctor Stallings meant to see him and John Lourdes dead.

TAMPICO, THE OLD town, was built during the time of the colonial viceroys. Arches and wrought-iron balconies, French scrollwork and imported English brick. The town reminded Rawbone of New Orleans, right down to the pure honey of satisfying the most private of pleasures.

The Southern Hotel was a five-story affair with elevators. It was a money house with a mahogany bar and café tables where you drank cocktails from real Tom Collins glasses. Businessmen stayed there, politicos, reporters from magazines like *Colliers* and *Saturday Evening Post*, men from the Klondike gold rush who came to wildcat for oil along the Panuco.

A key had been left for Rawbone at the hotel desk. When he entered the room, he was intensely troubled. The room was empty, but he could hear the shower running. He threw his bindle down on a bed. On the other was John Lourdes's shoulder holster, his carryall, his clothes . . . and that notebook.

In a flash of anger and resentment at having been gamed he grabbed the notebook and flung it. He did the same with the holster and carryall, even John Lourdes's clothes.

He realized that John Lourdes was besting him without even being in the room, without even being aware, just by being, just by . . .

His silhouette in the lamplight stiffened. He could hear himself warning: Remain indifferent, dammit. Lay it out for him. Doctor

Stallings . . . all you sense. Mr. Lourdes could write it all down in that sorry notebook.

He gathered up John Lourdes's things and put them back on the bed as they were. Walk away from this and everything that went with it, that was one possibility. Or find a way, a swift, sure way, to sacrifice John Lourdes and so save himself.

As he threw the pants on the bed, the wallet fell from the back pocket to the floor. He cursed as he bent to retrieve it. Spotting this sliver of gold visible from between the leather flaps, he spread the wallet open to be contemptibly sure it was what he thought it was. What lay on the cracked and dry leather surface—an insignificant trinket of a crucifix with one broken cross beam.

How long had it been since anything had savaged his being or left him bare? But there it was.

Was it possible—

He slipped the cross back and closed the leather flaps and put the wallet back in the pant pockets. He stood in the midst of upheaval knowing . . . he had been undone by his own hand.

IN THE ROOM, alone, John Lourdes dressed in clean clothes. He took his wallet from the other trousers. He made sure his mother's cross was there before tucking it into his back pocket. He slipped on his shoulder holster. He sat at a desk and prepared a wire to Justice Knox, then a letter to Wadsworth Burr.

Night had come and he motorcycled back out to the Agua Negra field offices to find out what had happened to Rawbone, but no one knew. While he was there John Lourdes did learn the women had been taken to a cafeteria for the guards down the road. That was to be their station. There he was told that Teresa and Sister Alicia had been brought to the mayor's house to work as part of the kitchen crew. He motorcycled to that address, which was by the Laguna del Carpintero.

The turreted house stood three stories in the moonlight. It was an ill-conceived spectacle of iron grillwork and marquees and Moorish porticos. In the huge lot behind it were two oil derricks, and where the ground declined toward the laguna was a foul black soup. There were piles of rotted lumber and a wrecked barge at the edge of the shore and supply shacks and chalans and a rusting truck with a fence around it for horses and mules and a battery of goats.

The house burned with light when John Lourdes rode past. In the great room with sconces and braided scrollwork were a dozen men. They were deep in conversation while drinking. One of the men was Doctor Stallings, another Anthony Hecht. John Lourdes parked the motorcycle against a tree and shadowed the darkness to get a better view.

The mayor, who was of Mexican descent, seemed to have much of the conversation directed at him, though there was one other man who appeared to be of central importance. He wore a near-white suit and favored a mustache much like John Lourdes. He was older and had a cultured face and often he would clip his thumbs inside his suspenders when he spoke.

Where the kitchen light cast itself upon the darkness John Lourdes saw a crew of women at their work stations. Teresa was in a corner scrubbing pots; Alicia was at the stove. He called to the old woman through the screen door. She put out her arms in a gesture of surprise at seeing him, then looked back at the closed door to the hall. They talked for a few minutes before she went and tugged at Teresa's hair.

Teresa came forward in a leather apron tied around her neck that hung almost to the ground; her arms were dripping wet. She was embarrassed yet elated at seeing John Lourdes. He held out a piece of paper torn from his notebook.

He had written: *I wanted to make sure you were alright. I'm staying at the Southern Hotel, if you find yourself with trouble.*

He wanted her to have it, but she made a gesture with her hand for the pencil. She slipped open the screen door. She wrote on the same page: *It's good to see you.* This she underlined.

From back in the house a man was calling out and the door to the hall swung open. John Lourdes forced the page they had written on into her hands before retreating to the darkness. In those few moments with Teresa he had picked up some of the conversation coming from that other room. Most of it seemed to deal with the mayor and where he stood politically now that the insurrection had been authorized.

Along the side of the house John Lourdes spotted a root cellar. It was practically beneath the rooms where the men were. He went and knelt by the canted entranceway. He looked about. There were but two men down by the derricks. He could see the faint glow of their cigarettes. He worked the latch and lifted the weathered door. He bent and felt his way down a set of wobbly steps. He closed the night off and hunched there in the dark. The cellar was foul with decay and fungaled shorings, the floor was flooded with a few inches of tainted water and every cautious step he took slopped behind him.

On the floorboards overhead the men's boots tapped out their pacings or creaked when chairs were moved. But that black and stinking hole was near about as good as a stethoscope for picking up their conversation.

THIRTY-ONE

WHEN HE LEFT the hotel room Rawbone walked the streets with his bindle slung over one shoulder like some aimless tramp. He tried to discredit every incident, every day, every hour and minute from El Paso to that very moment as if to deny the undeniable.

"There are times, Mr. Lourdes, when you say something and it's like you've known me all my life."

"Or maybe all my life."

Could it be John Lourdes doesn't know I am his father? He tried to convince himself of that possibility. That the young man in the Southern who was his son, his blood, might somehow have eradicated a father from memory. It was ridiculous and demanded raw stupidity to be even remotely believed. And the fact he was reaching that far enraged him, for it signaled weakness and fear and shame and how truly he'd been plowed under by the truth.

He stopped and looked in a shop window. His image there tinc-
tured by gas lamps. He removed the derby and cradled back his hair. He
was searching for his son, but his son was in that hotel room, he was a
member of the Bureau of Investigation, he was the man who had taken
him down, who he had traveled with for days, who had outplotted him,
who he'd brought to the women wracked with pain, who controlled
his fate. And who, only a faint hour ago, he had considered murdering.
John Lourdes was also the man who had never once acknowledged the
fact they were father and son. Suddenly the hearse came back to him,
when they had spoken to each other through its glass casement. He
stepped away from the window, unable to bear the sight of himself.

It was a weekend night. The streets were alive and rowdy with
horse-drawn trolleys and carriages flush with tourists. There were couples and laughter and people on balconies playing cards or listening
to Victrolas. Vendors sold ice cream and bottled mineral water and
candied treats. And Rawbone walked amongst all this alone and in the
possession of a shattering immensity.

John Lourdes had even changed his name. Probably, Rawbone
thought, for the same reason I had changed my own—shame. At least
we had that in common. The very idea of it caused bitter laughter that
verged on tears.

He walked the beach. He watched the tide roll in and foam over
the oily sand, he watched it fall away. He stood in the amber mist of the
casinos along the boardwalk.

His wife had hung that cross from a nail beneath a postcard of
Lourdes with a child standing before a statue of the Virgin Mary.
Rawbone had told her, "I hope she does a lot better for you than she
did for her own kid."

She'd been praying for her husband's conversion to goodness.
Deriding such an act, he had fired at the crucifix, shattering part of one
cross beam.

She'd picked it up from the floor and stood before him in that smoky hovel they called home. She pointed to each cross beam. The one that survived, the one that was shattered. "One for each thief crucified with Christ," she said. "Which do you want to be? These are the only choices for us all."

In a sparkflash he understood how John Lourdes had come by his name. He turned from the Gulf. How quickly it all had gone. From the casino an orchestra played. Through tall French doors he could see elegantly dressed ladies and gentlemen dance to the rich and soothing strings of a waltz.

He stood on the boardwalk in unrealized bereavement, then, disregarding the obvious, he opened a set of the French doors and entered the ballroom. He took off his derby and set it and his bindle on an empty table.

People soon took notice of this unshaven and road-filthy vagabond with an automatic in his belt. He looked about the room until his eyes fell upon a small group of women standing alone and listening to the music. They saw him approaching and whispered amongst themselves. There was one lady amongst them near about his own age with raven hair and Mediterranean skin.

"Pardon me," he said.

She turned and faced this strange man uncertainly.

"Would you have one dance with me?"

Her companions stared in disbelief.

"I know," he said, "how I look. But I can act the gentleman, and am a fine dancer."

Whatever the reason, be it rebellion or reserve, she agreed. He escorted her past stares and whispers.

Then there they were, waltzing to a grace of chords outside existence. They could have been any man and any woman in the ineffable light of what's possible, but they were not. She watched his face, unhurried and without judgment. He was a depiction of personal anguish and soon tears collected at the corners of his eyes.

"Sir," she said, "you're—"

"Yes . . . I saw my son for the first time today in almost fifteen years."

"You must be very happy."

"I abandoned him and his mother. She was dark like yourself. She has been dead since before I knew better."

This sudden and unexpected glimpse into someone's soul left her self-conscious. She tried to say something helpful.

"Maybe your son can forgive you this?"

"No, you see . . . my son also knows I am a common assassin."

The dancing stopped. He saw her confusion laced with fear. He thanked her, then walked away.

JOHN LOURDES SAT at a café table outside the Southern. He had three men under surveillance and was writing in his notebook when the father returned. He whistled and flagged him over. "Where have you been?"

The father sat. "Dancing, Mr. Lourdes."

The son leaned toward him. "Three men by the entrance. One is in a white suit."

The father had been studying the face of this stranger sitting next to him in the light of the new reality. He then glanced up through a row of candlelit faces to where three men crowded together over their whiskey glasses.

"The one in the white suit," said John Lourdes, "is named Robert Creeley. He is part of the U.S. Consulate here in Mexico. The men with him . . ." John Lourdes referenced his notes, ". . . are named Hayden and Olsen. They have adjoining suites to Creeley. I don't know what they do."

The father again took to staring at his flesh and blood.

"I bribed a desk clerk . . . with some of your money."

"Very practical," said the father.

"Those three were at the mayor's house tonight with a number of other men. Two of them . . . Doctor Stallings and Anthony Hecht."

Rawbone sat back. Stallings. He could feel the man's presence hovering over this very moment. The candle on the table flickered abstractly. He stared into its flame.

"Did you hear me?"

"I heard," said the father.

"What happened with Stallings?"

Rather than answer, the father asked, "What were you doing at the mayor's house?"

"Stallings had sent the girl there with the old woman to work. I went to see if they were alright. Men, over a dozen, were having some heated talk. All of them together. What does it mean?"

John Lourdes had been asking himself, but the father answered. "It means the Cains are getting ready to team up against Abel."

The statement was pointed yet cryptic and John Lourdes wanted to question Rawbone about it when the desk clerk walked over. "Mr. Lourdes," he said, "the phone call you've been expecting."

He thanked the man and slipped him some money. "Let's go," he said. The father stood, finished the last of John Lourdes's beer and followed. There was a telephone off the hook at the desk. John Lourdes answered and listened and soon he began to write in his notebook.

The father waited off to one side by the bar. From there he could watch Creeley and the other two. He was calculating how to proceed and whether to tell the son the truth about the conversation he'd had with the good doctor. He knew it would be determinative for John Lourdes.

He turned his attention to the son. All the years wondering what the moment of their meeting would be and it had already taken place in an El Paso lobby. "Keep your eyes at gunsight level," he'd said, "if you mean to make something of yourself . . ."

John Lourdes finished the call. "Truck close by?"

"Close by."

"Get it and meet me out front."

John Lourdes was on the street with shotgun and satchel when the truck pulled up. He climbed in. Rawbone noted the shotgun. The son had their destination written out in his notebook. "The Arbol Grande. Know it?"

"I know it."

He drove the tramway road. Marking their way the graying powdered smoke from the huge stacks of the Standard Oil Refinery. On the drive John Lourdes laid out what he'd overheard from that murky root cellar. The mayor of Tampico was receiving death threats because of his allegiance to the present regime. He was pleading for more support and protection. And the way he laid out these demands was no less than a veiled threat, his survival paralleling that of the oil fields, as both were vulnerable to acts of violence. He also insinuated the new regime might well have a different worldview of the oil companies and how they might be treated or taxed. He could not guarantee, under those conditions, the same kind of favorable treatment. Often, he used the phrase "direct American intervention" as the means of security and control.

Creeley, the gentleman at the Southern, told the mayor a case for American intervention had to be built carefully, and to that end, he added, unofficially, an investigation on the ground could well be in the works.

Rawbone heard it all, and cold hard reason told him no good would come of this. It smelled of Cuba. And Manila. And the law of a black argument. All he said was, "The shotgun."

John Lourdes glanced at the shotgun across his lap. "We're going to meet someone tonight about the weapons."

THIRTY-TWO

ALONG THE PANUCO everything seemed touched by smoke from the refineries. The buildings packed in along the shore as far as one could see were shrouded in gloom. The tramway crossed a channel that connected the laguna to the Panuco. The country there was wild and dark. John Lourdes took the flashlight from his carryall and the notebook in his hand flared up.

"This is the place."

The truck pulled off into the high reeds. Rawbone sat there vexed and checked his automatic. "Who contacted you?"

"Would it make a difference what name they used?"

The question went to the very core of their being.

"No."

They sat quietly for a bit.

"Why us, for this?" said the father. "Have you asked yourself that?"

"I have."

"And why didn't the good doctor just give us the weapons? To be delivered right off. Have you asked yourself that?"

"I have."

"And do you have an answer in your gunsights?"

"No . . . but I believe the answer may have me in its gunsights."

The son shut off the light and lit a cigarette. The father got out of the truck. They waited.

"You were raised in El Paso, were you not, Mr. Lourdes?"

"I was."

"The barrio?"

"The barrio."

He could not see the son from where he'd walked to in the high reeds. There was only the glow from the tip of John Lourdes's cigarette.

"There was a factory," Rawbone said casually, "that sewed American flags. I had a place a few doors up a walking street. Do you know it . . . the factory?"

"I seem to recall it."

"It's only an alley now for telephone poles. There's a pawnshop on one corner and a gun seller on the other where I picked up this Savage the day before we had . . . the good fortune . . . of stumble-fucking into each other."

He hesitated. There was only the sound of the water slipping down through the channel to the river and the Gulf beyond. As a man, the father felt completely boarded up, the shell that waited upon the wrecking ball.

"My wife is dead, but I have a son. What do you think, Mr. Lourdes? When I get back to El Paso . . . Do I try to find him? You know me. What I am. What do you think of the idea?"

The ash on the tip of the cigarette branded the dark intensely but never moved, never wavered. It held steady as a star in the night sky.

"I wouldn't answer, myself, Mr. Lourdes. A Chinaman is right. Silence is golden. Except, of course, when you're broke."

They went back to waiting amongst the brittle dry weeds. Each man alone in the wilderness of his existence. From the laguna came the sound of an engine. They could hear it turn into the canal.

"Tom Swift and his motor boat," said the father, "on lake whatever the hell it was."

John Lourdes flung away his cigarette. He got out of the truck. He turned the flashlight toward the canal. A voice in Spanish called out, "Jefe."

John Lourdes answered and the engine cut off as it slipped to shore.

John Lourdes approached the canal with Rawbone a few paces off his flank. From the boat one man came ashore, another remained onboard. The man introduced himself. His name was Mazariegos. He had a pointed face and whittled eyes and he spoke the king's English. John Lourdes let the beam drift over the boat long enough to recognize the man onboard as being the mayor, and that fact he whispered to Rawbone.

Mazariegos carried a lantern. Before he started discussing an arrangement he wicked up the flame and held the light aloft. From beyond the tramway bridge three horsemen came forward out of the reeds. They disappeared into the shadowline of the canal, then lifted up out of the willows on the near shore, their horses snorting and shaking off the wet. The men were rurales and heavily armed.

Mazariegos was there to oversee the discussions, but since both John Lourdes and Rawbone spoke fluent Spanish the talks became direct and unshaded. The price of the munitions had been settled by others, this was about where and when. "Where" was determined to be the head of the laguna at the place it fed into the canal. The campesinos would bring boats, as boats would give them ample routes of escape should there be trouble.

"When" was the following night. John Lourdes was in the process of agreeing when Rawbone interceded. He wanted it to be three nights from now, as extra time was imperative to ensure a safe delivery. Both sides were adamant, so it was left to Mazariegos to bring about a compromise of two nights hence.

"THE MAYOR DEMANDS protection," said Rawbone. "So Doctor Stallings guarantees his security against the very people the mayor is dealing munitions to."

They were by the truck after all had left, son and father. What one could not surmise, the other was sure of.

"Mr. Lourdes, you're either not seasoned enough or not cynical enough."

"Given enough selfishness and disdain I'm sure I can measure up to your standard."

"You're missing the point, Mr. Lourdes."

"Am I?"

The father came to him. He took the son by the vest collar in a scornful but gentlemanly way. "Mr. Mayor . . . I can solve both our problems. I want you to put out the word. I'll get you weapons. You get those campesinos to think you're quietly on their side. Put on your best political face. After you deliver them, we'll cut their fuckin' heads off. How does that sound, Mr. Lourdes?"

"It sounds . . . possible."

"If only the turkey could read a calendar, there'd be no Thanksgiving. Mr. Lourdes, you told me you heard the mayor making veiled threats out of one side of his mouth while asking for protection out of the other. He's a walking conflict of interests. I say they have the mayor in their gunsights. The practical application of strategy . . . they mean to have order and they're making a case for intervention. The oil fields are too valuable to the future."

Rawbone drove back to the Southern while John Lourdes sat beside him in silent council with his thoughts. Along the tramway, when they'd pass the occasional light from some roadside building, Rawbone would study the man who was his son. The child he'd squandered had defied the crime of chance. He had not been despoiled or destroyed by the laws of a vile gravity.

They entered the Southern lobby. It was down to the nighthawks now and the couples tucked away in quiet corners. A gentleman played piano softly in the bar. Rawbone stopped halfway through the lobby and took John Lourdes's arm so they could talk a moment.

"Walk out of here. Away from this. You've done it. All that was required and more. This is a quagmire, Mr. Lourdes. And it will never end like you think. Whatever I am, I know the world."

Rawbone went to the bar and ordered 100 proof drinkin' whiskey. He sat alone in the moody dark. He had come to a place in his own life he could not have fathomed. A place he could neither admit nor exceed. The son would never acknowledge him and he would not break faith with that. He would prove himself, he would hold to it, not because it was right or wrong, but because John Lourdes had willed it and he would match him will to will.

As a water glass with a lethal dose of liquor was placed before him, money was thrown upon the bar. He looked to find John Lourdes easing onto the seat beside him. The father looked furrowed in a manner the son had not seen before.

"We could have made tomorrow night," said the son. "Why did you want the extra days?"

The father sipped at the whiskey. Then, setting the glass, said, "I was hoping to buy you time to change your mind."

The son crossed his arms on the mahogany bar. He looked at the father through the glass behind the bottles.

"Mr. Lourdes, a hundred years from now there will be two gents sitting like we are now. One may be a federal agent for the Bureau of Investigation like yourself, the other may be a common assassin like yours truly, and they'll be in another Manila, or another Mexico. And they will be facing the same poison we are.

"There are two governments now, Mr. Lourdes. There is one that controls the White House, and there is one that controls the rest."

John Lourdes half turned. He reached for the father's glass. He drank.

"Mr. Lourdes, do you think they'd actually let the munitions be delivered?"

"Not on their lives."

John Lourdes set the glass down. The father had picked up an attitude in the son's voice, a glimmer in the way he stared. Aye, Rawbone recognized it, alright. It was a piece of himself. The piece meant to defy the laws of men, it had somehow broken through the birth canal and made its way into John Lourdes's soul. "They have a name for what you're thinking . . . you could call it madness . . . you could call it intervention . . . but it sure is not what Justice Knox had in mind."

The son's fingers brushed against his stubbled chin. His mind was tracking some private reserve. "What is required . . . but to do justice."

"Mr. Lourdes, take the Lord's Prayer and tie it around your neck and you'll find out it won't keep you from hanging."

The son leaned in close now to the father, so close they were near to being one. "I heard you by the canal," he said.

The father felt his guts cinch.

"And I heard you when we were sitting outside earlier slip around answering what Stallings talked about after I left."

"That."

"I'm going to hurt you in a way you could never imagine."

"Well, Mr. Lourdes, that would be a feat."

John Lourdes stood. "I'm going to put my faith in you. Not as an agent for the Bureau of Investigation . . . but as a man. That's how I'm going to hurt you."

John Lourdes took the father's glass and drank it empty then set the glass upside down on the bar. "Finito, jefe."

He took up his carryall and shotgun and started out.

"Mr. Lourdes."

He turned.

"You've never once called me by my name. I've kept mark. Never once."

"And I never will."

The father nodded. "Fair enough."

THIRTY-THREE

A STORM BLEW IN from the Gulf that night. By the next morning the tide swept over the breakers and sandbars and the river turned too rough for traffic. Down from the Southern, along the Panuco wharfs, was an open-air market that went on for blocks. Many of the stalls were covered with corrugated roofs. Rawbone stood out of the rain by a vendor who sold coffees and teas that could be laced with home-brewed mescal. He was waiting on Doctor Stallings, who now approached down that muddy causeway.

He wore a long black slicker and his umbrella was angled against the sheeting rain. Rawbone was leaning against a post and sipping from a steamy cup when Doctor Stallings joined him. Neither man spoke. Stallings shook the wet from his umbrella and then closed it up. He asked, "Are you going to tell me about last night?"

Rawbone drank but did not answer.

The rain came down in sheets across the corrugated roof, creating that hard drum echo, and from the fires to heat the coffee and fight the damp the air was misty and flueish.

Rawbone finally answered Doctor Stallings. "Back at the train you said something that stayed with me."

"We're here to talk about—"

"Grandeur and finality," said Rawbone. "That was it. Yeah. We'll cover last night. But first . . . let's talk finality."

JOHN LOURDES SAT at his hotel room desk and folded up a letter for the man who was his father. He looked out upon the riled waters of the Panuco as he awaited Rawbone's return. That morning he had taken to the motorcycle, challenging the rains. He'd driven the oil fields with their soaking and grime-stained laborers, and their women in tarpaper cafeterias and stifling warehouses, and Indians on rickety carretas and junker wagons relegated to the lowest scraps of work. They existed under the guidon of imposed fealty. A stranglehold of the futile and the feudal that was, in fact, what had brought his mother to America. It was why she'd ridden boxcars and walked bleached wastes to cross the Rio Grande and stand naked in that fumigation shed all to reach the promise of freedom and opportunity.

He was thinking of his mother as he sat on that idling motorcycle in the rain atop the same rise where Díaz and his surrogates stood in that film, and used it to lie to the world about the state of their nation. And John Lourdes, under a rolling thunder, came to see how much he was his mother's journey. He was not only the agent of her hopes but the eternal argument of her trials toward that freedom and opportunity.

Lightning flashed across the window as John Lourdes slipped his notes into the envelope with the letter, then set it down on the desk. He drank a beer and smoked and watched the harbored storm until the door lock turned.

Rawbone took his sodden hat and put it on the bureau. He hung his coat on the closet door. He went and sat in a cushioned chair in the far corner, all without a word.

"Is it the mayor?" said John Lourdes.

The father answered in a guarded tone, aware of the effect what he was about to say would have. "We are to pick up the munitions at dusk. We are to deliver them to the appointed place at the appointed time. We are to kill the men who come for them. We are then to go to the mayor's house. I am told there is a carriage barn on the property. We are to put the munitions there—"

"What?"

"We are to put the munitions there. The mayor will be at home. We are to kill him. We are to kill anyone and everyone in the house, to leave no witness to that fact."

They sat now with the knowing. Rain spattered across the window. Drops that seemed to carry the weight of time.

"I believe Doctor Stallings sent those women to work at the house knowing full well what he had in mind. Their actions in the desert marked them. And you also. Our friend the doctor asked if I could fully trust you."

John Lourdes sat back. "And what did you say?"

"That I could only fully trust myself."

John Lourdes thought through the situation. "You were giving him clearance to put a bullet through my head."

"Would you have handled it any differently?"

John Lourdes shook his head no. It was, after all, a practical application of strategy.

"If the girl's welfare means something to you, get her out. Then strike it from here, Mr. Lourdes. You've exceeded what's expected."

John Lourdes stood. He took the envelope and walked across the room and set it on the bed against the father's bindle.

"What is that?"

"A letter to Justice Knox. I had it notarized so there'd be no question as to its authenticity. My notes are in there also."

The father took a long breath. He eyed the letter.

"I put the film I took from the funeraria in your bindle."

"My bindle?"

The father leaned out from the chair and took the envelope but hesitated opening it. Rather, he looked up at the son with a frank stare.

"The letter says you've earned your immunity. I need to make sure my notes get back. I'm leaving that to you."

The father tried to absorb and understand. "Last night in the bar. I get it now."

John Lourdes walked back to the desk. He reached for the open beer and drank.

"Mr. Lourdes, why are you doing it?"

John Lourdes took to looking out the window. "You've earned it. And I'm staying."

"That's not what I asked. And you know it, Mr. Lourdes."

How does he explain without explaining himself? Or a deaf girl who in a few simple phrases spoke to a pure forgiveness. How does he open up about the woman that man across the room abandoned, for whom there was no grievance so great that she could not forgive, because the eternal, not the ephemeral, was her preeminent star? And how does he explain that place inside him where the common assassin who sat amongst the dead listening to a lullaby and the rogue who kidnapped alligators to keep them from freezing in the Texas cold held out in the absence of everything, refusing to die?

"Mr. Lourdes . . . why are you doing it?"

Turning, John Lourdes, his face and voice resolute, answered, "As long as you live, don't ever ask me that. Now . . . take the letter and leave."

The father looked down at the envelope. He had been fundamentally emptied, having now in his hands exactly what was necessary, but nothing else. The son was right. He had hurt him in a way the father never imagined.

"As you say, Mr. Lourdes."

ONCE ALONE, JOHN Lourdes leveled his focus on the force of dark tides he was about to confront. He left the room to make sure the truck was right, with enough gasoline and extra parts for an escape. After nightfall he drove in the rain to the mayor's house and waited amongst the dripping trees. When Sister Alicia went from the kitchen to a smokehouse by that rusting truck, he made a stealthy approach. Coming upon the unsuspecting woman, he put a hand to her mouth to keep hush. He had a note for her and Teresa and made her swear they tell no one. They must believe and wait.

Sleep was impossible. He went from one black scenario to another, planning out a strategy for survival, and all the while the shadow of the father was with him in thought, word and deed.

There was no dawn, only rain. There was no sun, only a gravel sky. There was no dusk, only a spreading mist.

The truck was parked in an alley behind the Southern. John Lourdes set his carryall on the cab floor, his shotgun and rifle within reach. He kicked the engine over and tossed his cigarette, then shifted into gear and started up the alley through a runny fog toward the street. His mind was at gunsight level when the man who was his father stepped from a last doorway.

Rawbone stood before the truck in silhouette. John Lourdes braked and draped his arms over the wheel. The father came around to the driver's side of the cab and in a quiet voice said, "Mr. Lourdes, I know who I am . . . and I know who you are. I am asking . . . save a seat in the truck for me."

The muscles along the son's cheeks made a sudden and unexpected flinch. He knew, without exception, this moment would never be again. It would flee every chance, escape any wish, if he did not grasp it now. Without a word John Lourdes slid across the seat. The father tossed his worldly goods on the cab floor and climbed in behind the wheel and drove.

THIRTY-FOUR

THE ROAD THROUGH the oil fields was grouted in mud, the derricks mere speculations in the mist. The Agua Negra compound was quiet, save for a handful of station guards. Authorization was already in hand for independent contractors to pick up the makings of an icehouse. But in this case there were no bills of lading, no paper trail of signatures, no receipts that shipment had been received in good order. The process was faceless, the loading of the truck a tired repetition.

The father asked John Lourdes how this night was supposed to play out. John Lourdes said he had already forewarned the women with the note telling them to be ready for tonight and leaving and that their survival depended on it. Once there, he would warn the mayor, get him out. He would then deliver the weapons and hope to flee Tampico with his own life.

"You were right," added the son.

"About?"

"Exactly what worried Justice Knox. Me. My character where it concerned . . . the practical application of strategy."

Rawbone was now staring into the lifeline of his own child. "The world is a tricky place, Mr. Lourdes. It's mostly gestures and gratuities. So I'd wait in judgment on myself."

John Lourdes glanced at the father. "You're trying to tell me something."

"I don't even whisper and you can hear me."

Tampico was shoring in mist. The river black and roily. Window light guided their truck through the darkened gray of the streets as the father went on. "When I was in Manila, insurgents had improvised explosives. They meant to bomb the funeral of an American general named Lawton. There were to be consuls there. Politicians, dignitaries. They wanted to create an incident. Isn't that what Stallings and the others are doing to make their case for intervention?"

"Where are you going with this?"

"The practical application of strategy . . . the women and the mayor may need to be dead."

EVERYTHING HAPPENED VERY quickly after that. While the son waited with the truck, the father walked the grounds with a shotgun. There was only a bare crew down by the derricks. They were hard cases but the father persuaded them at barrel point to "politely fuckin' remove themselves from the vicinity." When the son saw them scattering through the high weeds up the laguna, he sped forward.

They were in the house moments later. The cook screaming, the father demanding the mayor's whereabouts. While she told him he was in his private quarters showering, John Lourdes had Alicia gather up the women and get them onto the truck. Then he took Teresa by the hand and pulled her out of there.

The mayor near fainted when a rowdy with a shotgun burst into the bath where he showered. He looked like some stricken popinjay cowering there and covering up his noble parts. Reaching through the streaming water Rawbone grabbed the man by the hair and told him in no uncertain terms, "From the looks of you, that's the last thing you need to worry about protecting."

The mayor begged for his life with hands clasped while Rawbone dragged him through the bedroom, shouting over his pleas to explain what in the miserable hell was going on.

Five women and a valet were being packed up onto the truck when the screen door was kicked open, near coming off its hinges. Rawbone had the mayor in tow. He was still naked and barefoot but clung to a waistcoat and pair of pants. Dripping wet and shivering, he had to be pushed and booted up onto the truckbed.

Rawbone walked past the rig and opened the gate to the corral around the rusting truck and fired a double of shots into the air to chase off the goats and horses and mules. He shouted at that scattering menagerie, "You'll thank me one day, you filthy beggars."

He returned to the truck and dumped the shotgun on the cab seat then clapped his hands together and called out, "Got them for me?"

John Lourdes tossed him two wraps of dynamite he'd just finished binding together.

"Mr. Lourdes, get this damn parade out of here."

As the truck rumbled forward and swung about, teeter-tottering wildly, Rawbone lit one wrap and flung it into the kitchen. He then ran down to the derricks through all the oily slop. He lit the next fuse and set the bound sticks on the decking.

They had turned into the tramway road when the first explosion went off. Not a minute later the wells detonated and flames hollowed up through the mist maybe two hundred feet. The oil had ignited and a fuming black char began to billow over the rooftops and out upon the laguna. Rawbone yelled to the mayor who was trying desperately to worm into his trousers. "Hey, Alcalde . . . look at them flames. You and the witches here are now officially dead. How does it feel?"

THE SIGNAL WAS to be a lantern placed high on a stake where the laguna and the channel merged. The shoregrass was near high as a man and they hid there with the truck.

Because he meant to return to Texas, John Lourdes had written the address of Wadsworth Burr and the BOI headquarters so Teresa could let him know where she could be found.

Teresa was sixteen, going into the wilds with nothing. He felt a severe apprehension touched with farewell. He clutched her hand and what she felt there and saw in his face made her lean over and kiss him.

Rawbone called out through the dark, "Boats are coming!"

You could not see them; there was only this slow metronomic poling somewhere in the mist. John Lourdes put a finger to his ears and his eyes and pointed to the laguna. She understood and stretched up a bit to see. He still had her hand and she cupped the other over his and they remained like that until the boats appeared, flat and square, ferrying out of a deathly gray. She asked for his pencil and wrote: *I will find my way, as you will yours.*

While Rawbone walked to the shore to get a jump on explaining what they'd hidden there in the weeds, John Lourdes pulled out his wallet and took from it the crucifix. He put the gold memory in Teresa's hand and she was reminded of that first night in Juárez at the church when she wrote in his notebook. The moments to express anything more were vanishing as the chalans touched shore.

AT THE AGUA Negra compound Doctor Stallings received a report by phone of a derrick fire along the north shore of Tampico. A sudden foreboding came over him even as he asked where. He called together a squad of men under Jack B and they sped in touring cars to the site.

The house was near consumed, the derricks gone, the rusting truck in the backyard glowed with heat. Walls of flame turned and flagged as they breathed up air. The doctor was given a report by one of the derrick hands who'd been run off. He described a man with a shotgun and a derby whose description left little room for doubt.

Doctor Stallings had Jack B and part of the crew sweep the grounds and laguna looking for bodies. On the far side of the collapsing house was the carriage barn. It alone had been saved as the wind kept the flames from having at it. With faces hidden behind bandanas Stallings and a few men kicked open the latch doors. The barn was dark and gritted with smoke and Doctor Stallings could hear Rawbone in his head, "Let's talk finality."

THIRTY-FIVE

THEY HAD WATCHED the two flatboats disappear across a night sea and into a nacre mist with their cargo of munitions and women and a disheveled half-dressed mayor and his valet. "Yesterday he'd have staked out those campesinos if it meant survival. Tonight he's one of them. That . . . is a practical application of strategy. Mr. Lourdes . . . the mayor reminds me of me. Except for the noble parts."

John Lourdes waited and listened until the last whisper of those poling oars. He took the wheel now. Their destination, darkness and escape. They were justified in believing the advantage of time was on their side of the ledger, but a little bad luck and an ill wind had put them in play.

Doctor Stallings was already on the hunt. He called the field garrison and ordered crews of men in vehicles and on horseback to search the roads around Tampico for a three-ton truck with AMERICAN

PARTHENON painted on the side. Outlying pipeline stations and ware-house depots were alerted by telegraph to be on the lookout for two suspects in an act of possible murder and sabotage. As for the Mexican authorities, these Stallings waited to inform till he was certain of political advantage.

Son and father struck inland toward San Luis Potosí. A river of night stars appeared wondrously through the failing mist. In the bare light of a building along the pipeline the shifting truck gears drew a watchman's suspicions. He stood in the road while it rumbled past with Rawbone tipping his hat to the old man in a gesture of good evening.

Word was telegraphed, and with that a mandala of armed men was on the move. John Lourdes and Rawbone had dug up the small cache of weapons they'd hidden away. If they reached the city, their plan was to sell them to fund a run to the border.

They drove on through an expanding emptiness, the shadow of their rig running an ocean of creosote. Suddenly a spire rose burning skyward behind them.

"Mr. Lourdes, we've got the Fourth of July on us."

John Lourdes stopped the truck and came about in his seat. A trailing flare miles back, but before it died away another, well to the west, was fired into the air.

"We're being marked," said John Lourdes.

RAWBONE DROVE WHILE John Lourdes sat with flashlight and map, charting a new course of deceptions to cheat capture. But even in the dark the pursuit advanced, their flares marking the coal-black heavens, determined and absolute.

Son and father kept on through the black and wild night, hunted like nameless migrants, climbing up through lonely miles of piñon and chiseled rock. Along the battered remains of mining roads and mule trails, the truck managed the ascent like a slow and hulky beast toward vested cloudbanks. Along the crest they detonated the battened passage behind them to slow the pursuit. But even so, before dawn by a spring at the entrance to a stark plain they could see a retinue of lights traversing the darkened rock face in steady order. From there, a flare went up.

Son and father scanned the desert floor and in the country to their flank there came an answering flare, followed yet by a third atop the distant flats of a mesa. Their pursuers were closing in with the punitive resolve of some fabled deity.

While the father filled the water bags and gassed the truck from a drum, John Lourdes studied the map. But he saw they were beyond remedy now, so he tossed the map in that shallow waterway where it floated briefly before the ink ran, then paled, and the paper sank.

"It's here . . . or there."

The father looked out to where a cresset light rose over a day's run of hammered dust bordered by windless foothills.

"Take your choice, Mr. Lourdes."

"I say we make them earn our blood."

They pushed hard into an emptiness where the dark burned away and the earth reddened and the air choked you dry. Rawbone was in the back, mounting the .50 caliber on its tripod. He had rigged a tarp over part of the truckbed. Removing his derby, he wrapped a bandana around his head. John Lourdes whistled and the father turned.

To the west, thin ripples of smoke. A flare arrowed out toward where the truck was running. From behind them another. On their far flank another. The flares were gridding them and so the son looked back at the father. Their faces were harrowed and stained with red dust. It would be soon.

The first of them wheeled toward the truck. Three riders pitched forward in their saddles. Hard cases reeking with intent. Rawbone edged around the .50 caliber so the barrel sat over the sideboard with its AMERICAN PARTHENON streaked by the red clay of the desert floor.

Rawbone opened fire. A hail of dust and blood. The nightmare faces of the unsuspecting men, the horses wrenching sideways as they fell. The truck sped away, leaving this spot of earth looking as if it had vomited up death.

Spumes of dust in a closing arc. A flare missiled at the truck, struck the engine hood. Sparks everywhere burning John Lourdes's face and arms. He swapt at them with a hand and hat as if they were a swarm of torched bees.

The gunfire intensified. The .50 caliber shell casings spattered and dinged across the steel chassis. The riders closed in one surge. They pressed their mounts and fired at the tires. The truck zigged and straightened, then swerved and sent up rolling walls of gritted red that left the riders blind.

A punishing mile and the lathered mounts began to wane. The riders kept on but were falling back. Rawbone could just make out the dusty figures of Doctor Stallings and Jack B and he screamed to them over the barrel of that machine gun, "I'll write you ladies when I get settled."

They pressed on with the stencil of the truck long and sleek upon the earth. They were buying time for the hourglass when far ahead in the melting heat a floating illusion of water damn near shimmering like sunset. John Lourdes yelled to Rawbone to come about and he did . . . and was sure of nothing that he saw.

It appeared to be some vast standing lake that would blink and disappear as the ground dipped, then it would liquid back up out of the desert clay as the truck wheels climbed some hardened dune.

It was there, then gone, and then it was—

The truck braked. The men got out. They walked to the edge of that still and seemingly endless body of blood-colored water.

"The storm that came in from the Gulf," said John Lourdes.

"Dry lagoon . . . this'll be nothing by tomorrow."

Rawbone ran to the truck and grabbed the binoculars. John Lourdes looked up shore and then down. The damn thing stretched on for how far he could not tell. He stepped into the water to test its depth. Rawbone scanned the desert. That body of dust had broken into two widening wings.

"We've got just a couple of beers' worth of time before they get here."

He turned to find the son near forty yards on into that glassy red muck.

"How deep do you think it is at the worst?"

The father understood. "We get stuck out there—"

John Lourdes hurried to shore and hustled past the father and jumped into the truckbed.

"We're too heavy. And if the tires sink—"

John Lourdes was surveying what they carried. There were four drums of gasoline and a few crates of munitions. "Look across that lagoon," John Lourdes said. "You can see slips of land. It wasn't more than a few inches where I walked."

He'd grabbed a crate and spilled out its contents. He now tossed back in a few hand grenades, dynamite, a reel of cable, the detonator. He slid the crate to the father. "Put that up front."

He jumped from the truckbed and ran to the cab. He was on one side, the father the other.

"You're always one to throw around a remark," said the son.

"I pride myself on having a good wit."

John Lourdes pointed to the lagoon. "Do you think you could part the red sea for us?"

WITH RIFLE IN hand Rawbone loped ahead of the truck. Water spilled out through the slow-turning wheel wells and John Lourdes kept watch from the cab. Every time the truck sank or the tires spun he sweated out the moments till the reflection of the rig on what looked to be a pan of liquid fire rolled on.

Rawbone swung about and looked back. The advancing riders were no longer dust but men trampling down upon the phalanx of their shadows stretching out across the earth.

This was to be the hour. They swung the truck up onto an island of red clay in the heart of the lagoon. They plotted their defense. They protected the tires with crates. They rolled two drums of gasoline out from the truck until they were almost submerged. They knifed holes through the metal casings large enough to wedge in sticks of dynamite. They set the charges and ran the wire along the surface of the water to the detonator behind the truck. They would have the sun at their backs, and if they could survive to see nightfall they might yet steal away with their lives.

The oncoming battery of guards reached the edge of the lagoon. Doctor Stallings had one group under his command, Jack B the other. Stallings focused his binoculars. The truck sat sideways on a shell of ground. The words AMERICAN PARTHENON were streaked wet with red cake kicked up from the wheels, and imprinted like a coat of arms upon the water before it.

Doctor Stallings issued orders. The two wings of the assault started forward at a slow walk, the attackers feeling their way until that slow walk became an easy trot and Doctor Stallings lifted his arm and there was a volley of gunfire from their ranks followed by a storm of flares.

The shells exploded against the truck, above it, in the water before it. The air burned and stank, the sky discolored. John Lourdes huddled with the detonator, Rawbone in the truckbed with his face against the .50 caliber barrel. The riders veered to the flanks of the truck, closing, firing; another assault of flares followed. That small island now under a hellish rocket siege. Bursts of red glare, tracers spiraling off wildly on into the lagoon, sparks falling from the sky like smoking confetti.

Upon that barren plain futures met in a blinding instant. The shining sea around the truck erupted in a volcanic heaven of men and mounts and red rain. Horsemen consumed in flames like something out of an apocalyptic nightmare reached the island in the last moments of their existence with weapons extended from scorched arms. The second charge blew, and death's mouth opened with a force that consumed them all. The red rain fell. It fell through blazing streamers of fire and it fell through banks of black smoke rising in the windless air.

From amongst the carnage and the dead one man rose like an apparition without a shadow or a name. He stepped over an arm with its inked flag floating lifelessly, and alone he walked amongst the remnants of men and mounts scattered across the shallows and up onto that island of red clay where the truck still stood. There, beneath the words AMERICAN PARTHENON, lay John Lourdes.

THIRTY-SIX

THE FATHER STAGGERED past a fallen mount and came to his knees over the son. There was a bloody eyelet through the vest just below the ribs on the heart side, and also a matching hole in the back. But John Lourdes's eyes were open and he was breathing.

"Has it gone clear through?" came the halting voice.

"It has, Mr. Lourdes." Rawbone looked past the dead around him and the desolation beyond . . . survival, that's what he was searching for. "We've got to make clock, Mr. Lourdes."

He hastened to the truck. His being tightened as he kicked over the engine, unsure it would go. It started like a charm. He shifted gears and it went forward sluggardly.

"Mr. Lourdes . . . hear that . . . Parthenon here is gonna carry you home."

THE TRUCK CLIMBED the first altar of hills and shouldered along the skyline with a falling sun far to their west. Before them a world as it was at the time of creation.

John Lourdes lay on the cab seat facing a hard run of two days with barely enough water for the truck. Rawbone drove through the night with lanterns hung from the cab stanchions to light the way. He drove through dust that scored his eyes, and heat that dried them to the bone.

He watched the son weaken and yet refuse to drink. If there wasn't enough for one, there wasn't enough for the other. The father cursed him furiously, and John Lourdes answered, "We'll make it, or we won't."

They labored hugely over swells of white pumice and through un-reckonable granite canyons. John Lourdes's words came back to the father: "There is no past, there is no future . . . there is only you, and me, and this truck."

Even now it was a test of wills. His mouth dry and cracking, his eyes failing, in desperate need of water there on the seat he would not drink, the father said, "Mr. Lourdes, should I come knocking at your door one night in El Paso and offer to buy you dinner and drinks, what would you think?"

"I would think . . . you were paying for it with stolen money."

He had no strength to laugh, so a grunt had to suffice. "The Modern Café in the Mills Building lobby. The sight of our illustrious meeting. We'll drink gentleman's whiskey from Tom Collins glasses and toast surviving."

The muscles in Rawbone's body were breaking down; the night was no cooler than the day. He had kept a rock in his mouth to foster spit but even that was too little, too late. He remembered being a boy with nothing in a pawny waste called Scabtown and watching a fighter in the baking sun stalk an adversary. Even now, especially now, those battered and blood-streaked features once witnessed spoke to his fury and resolve.

By morning the sun was striking him down. His grip on the wheel slipped away and he momentarily passed out. He cursed himself and pressed on again. Sometime that morning they came upon a necklace of tiny pools. The father rushed to it desperately with a water bag only to discover with one taste it was alkali.

Poison.

He looked back at the truck. The tarp above the cab lifted uneasily with the breeze. His mind flashed on a funeral canopy—he killed the thought of it quickly. But he knew. They would be dust before the day was done.

He stared through the searing heat at the black surface of that pool, so utterly still, and came to a moment that was absolute and providential. He slipped the water bag into that bitter fountain and watched the bubbles reach the air and die away. He wondered, would the water taste of oblivion.

When the bag was full he stoppered it, then he leaned down and put his mouth to the pool and drank. He drank like some bloodthirsty drunk and sat with the tainted liquid spilling down his chin, and there in the watery slicks the common assassin and the father looked at each other for the last time.

He went to the truck, howling with good news they had water, and he drank from the bag and he tricked the son by handing him the other. The son drank the good water. "Close your eyes, Mr. Lourdes, and think of the Modern Café."

He punished the truck as he punished himself. Over every rise a hope that sinks in his throat with each trembling horizon. Memories threadbare with time are suddenly upon him with an emotional pull too heartrending to bear. He drives them from his mind. There is only surviving.

A flock of white-tailed doves streaks past overhead. Their presence is a promise of water. And if there is water—

They are like runes against the sky and he lets their flight guide his course as he begins to feel his body turn against him. He is counting every dusty heartbeat with each windy slope. With each mile he is being murdered, he is a mile closer to being saved. He keeps thinking of that blood-streaked fighter in the dust whose name he bears, and through a dazy heat he sees the stylus of a church spire against a flat sky and the town of San Luis Potosí that enfolds it.

IN THE SHADOW of the church was a small hospital run by nuns for the poor and dispossessed. Rawbone was already in the early throes of a convulsion when the truck crashed up on the sidewalk. This was the first moment a barely conscious John Lourdes realized something was drastically wrong.

Rawbone dragged himself to the stone wall and sat with his back against the hot brick, fighting for air. John Lourdes was in the arms of nuns and campesinos but he pulled and pleaded and finally broke loose as if they were somehow his captors and he crumpled up on the street beside the father. He grabbed his shoulders. "What . . . ?"

Rawbone tried to make words out of broken syllables or breathless sound, but could not. In his hand was the pocket notebook and, wracked and dying, he held it out for John Lourdes to see what he had written hours ago: Son—forgive me

John Lourdes was beyond the knowing, beyond asking, "How?" He was clinging to a furious history that was his life, desperate suddenly for what was inseparable and lost, trying to contain or hold back death, to overpower it with his heart.

But the father kept breaking apart. There was no will, no earthly force that can measure up, even the blood-streaked fighter in the dust could not ultimately stand against that most inevitable of adversaries.

John Lourdes pulled his father to him, grasping the hand with the notebook, and in that ephemeral moment with the blazing sun around them, they were one. The son whispered, "Yes . . . yes, I forgive you."

He could feel his father's face against his own and this choking sound through clenched teeth like, "Yes." Then the son put his lips to his father's ear, "Can you still hear me?"

The father squeezed his son's hand, answering that he could and his son told him, "Father . . . save a seat in the truck for me."

Somewhere in that poisonous fever the father filled with those words and then, through what seemed this twilight tunnel, he could have sworn he heard the truck engine and the gears shifting and the steel musculature picking up speed and he was riding with the son through a land that was neither desolate nor forsaken . . . and then he was no more.

THIRTY-SEVEN

THERE WERE JUST unanchored moments after that—being lifted from the sidewalk and the body against that ageless brick, the smell of ether and shadows upon an operating room wall. How long he was unconscious he did not know, but he came to in the dark, feeling as if he were on a train. His eyes followed a trail of light back to a kerosene lamp. A nurse sat nearby in the storage car, reading. She was Mexican and middle-aged and there was a solitary peacefulness about her. As she smiled at him, a figure leaned over the cot. It was Wadsworth Burr.

"Where are we?"

"You're on a train, John. I'm taking you to the military hospital at Brownsville. It was your notebook. The nuns saw my address and notified me."

"My father—"

"John, just listen, right now. This is imperative. When Justice Knox comes to see you, you're to say nothing unless I'm in the room. Do you understand? Nothing."

John Lourdes was swimmy and confused.

"A politician in Tampico was allegedly murdered and there is a suggestion you were somehow involved."

What surprised Wadsworth Burr was that John Lourdes laughed. It was gravelly and ironic and self-possessed, it was a laugh he had heard before.

THE HOSPITAL WAS on the Fort Brown military post. The window in John Lourdes's room looked out toward the Resaca. At night the soldiers would play cards along the shore in the lamplight. John Lourdes spent the weeks there recuperating fundamentally alone. He had a masculine thirst for silence and used it to revisit his life and the fallen adversary that had become again his father.

Justice Knox arrived with a stenographer. Burr was present as John Lourdes accurately detailed the events in Mexico, which were corroborated in his notes, even down to turning the munitions over to a group of campesinos. The only fact overlooked—his being the son of that common assassin.

The front of the hospital had a long covered portico with brick archways where one could avoid the searing Texas sun. Justice Knox excused the stenographer, and he and Wadsworth Burr started down that walkway alone.

"He'll have to resign."

"Oh," said Wadsworth Burr, "at the very least."

Burr took a cigarette case from his coat pocket. "The notes my client sent to you. A copy was also sent to me. I immediately hired detectives in Mexico to begin my own investigation. Cigarette?"

Knox shook his head no. This news did not sit well. There was a bench nearby where Burr went.

"A man named Tuerto was hired by Doctor Stallings through Agua Negra to photograph the oil fields, wharfs, river, harbor, rail lines."

"Which sounds like a useful policy for a security firm."

Burr crossed his legs and lit the cigarette. "I have a signed affidavit from this Mr. Tuerto that he delivered copies of the photographs to Mr. Robert Creeley, who as you know from John's notes and briefing, or your own investigation, is adjunct to the U.S. consulate in Mexico."

"There is nothing extraordinary about that either. The oil companies, as well as others, have been making their case about field security since the first hints of a revolution."

"Mr. Creeley was staying at the Southern. The same hotel as my client . . . clients. As were two other gentlemen, Olsen and Hayden. Who, as you probably know through your own investigation, as I do through mine, are information gatherers for the Department of State."

Justice Knox had been standing under an archway, but now he went and sat at the far end of the same bench as Wadsworth Burr. "I know where you're going. The meeting at the house."

"You have an official of the U.S. consulate. Field officers for the Department of State. An American businessman procuring illegal munitions. A former Ranger heading a security firm for the oil companies receiving that shipment of munitions."

"Creeley, Hayden, and Olsen," said Justice Knox, "all acknowledge they were invited to a dinner by the mayor, as was Doctor Stallings. The mayor, for his part, wanted to make the case for American military protection. The oil companies are a significant tax base for him. Hecht denies being at the meeting. Creeley and the others state he was not there. As for the munitions, Hecht says he helped smooth the way for a shipment he was told was the parts of an icehouse to be delivered to the oil fields. He denies even knowing Stallings."

"I have in my possession a film," said Burr, "one of those newsreels Díaz shot to advertise the grand achievements of his administration, though they were, in fact, a tome of aggrandizement to his royal self. It shows clearly that Hecht and Stallings were acquainted."

"Stallings is dead."

"You have my client's statement about what transpired."

"I have your client's statement he delivered munitions to a group intent on overthrowing the government."

"You don't think you're going to get to pick and choose which of these statements are fact and which are not? You're going to have to deal with the whole body of evidence."

Justice Knox looked into that pale stare. Burr was frail. The way he crossed his legs seemed at times effeminate. But he was not subject to intimidation.

Burr sat quietly for now. He looked out upon the Resaca and a line of troops going about their drills on the dusty parade grounds. He blew on the tip of his cigarette, which pulsed intensely while he considered, then considered further, before he spoke.

"I'm going forward on the basis that you're an honest man. Knowing full well honest men, sometimes the most honest, are in positions of default. The evidence, even as you lay it out, favors two possibilities. Because the munitions themselves can never be separated from the facts.

"One possibility . . . the men at the meeting were part of an attempt to make a case for military intervention. Possibly heightening or exaggerating the evidence to make such a case. We might even conclude that Doctor Stallings was a rogue element working independently for such an end.

"The other possibility . . . in that meeting they were not making a case for intervention, they were creating a case for intervention. And they were not beyond using the most nefarious of methods to achieve such an end. And you know what that can lead to. Coup d'état . . . assassination."

Burr rose and walked to the archway. His sunken features were intently grave. "I do not envy your position. The public discussion of such matters would put you at the center of a controversy. That is the perfect battlefield for an attorney, but not the head of the BOI, who represents not only his organization, but the government of Texas as well."

While they faced each other a nurse pushing a wheelchair passed by. The patient, missing an arm and a leg, wasn't much more than thirty. He saluted both men in an offhanded manner. The wheels definitely needed oiling and when that sound was far down the shaded walkway, Burr said, "I've been told many of the permanents here served in Manila and Cuba. Was that war worth it?"

"We're not discussing that war."

"But we are in discussion."

Justice Knox acknowledged that with a nod. He took off his glasses and rubbed at the pinch marks the frames left on his nose. Burr already recognized from previous meetings the gesture meant he was troubled and needed time to think.

"I should never have sent John."

"The practical application of strategy," said Burr.

"It's not a question of his courage or dedication."

"I know your worldview. The practical application of strategy has its place. But taken to an ultimate end do you know what else it can be?" Burr paused for a half breath to accent his point. "It's Washington not crossing the Delaware . . . it's Lincoln not freeing the slaves."

Wadsworth Burr took a last quiet draw on his cigarette then crushed it under the heel of his finely made shoes. "I will wait to hear where your thoughtful and, I'm certain, difficult deliberations take you before I determine a course of action for my client."

JOHN LOURDES AND Wadsworth Burr returned to El Paso by train a month later. John Lourdes had received word he would be given a letter of commendation for "his dedication in uncovering the illegal shipment of arms to a foreign country." On that day, at that hour, the commendation and all it said and did not say was, to John Lourdes, mere dust in the wind.

They drove in Burr's Cadillac from his home to Concordia Cemetery. Burr had taken it upon himself to have Rawbone brought back to Texas and buried beside John Lourdes's mother. The headstone was simple. It had his name and a bookmark of dates. The cemetery was on a flat plain, rough and with a few trees. The sky was crisp blue that day but the cemetery seemed so much more spare than John Lourdes even remembered.

He stood there thinking, long and hard, on the deeply flawed and tragic history that was his father. A sweep of feelings went through him. Feelings he would have sworn unimaginable this lifetime. Loss above all, loss unfathomably raw, that reached to the very roots of his blood.

"There was more of him in me," admitted John Lourdes, "than I ever imagined. Or would have ever believed."

Burr nodded, then after a brief consideration, said, "It appears there was much more of you in him, than he might ever have imagined."

With that, they started from the gravesite. Upon reaching the car, John Lourdes took a moment and glanced back at the grave, then toward the Rio Grande and the red cut mountains beyond.

EPILOGUE

IN 1913 THE U.S. ambassador to Mexico, Henry Lane Wilson, was involved in plotting the coup d'état that overthrew the Madero government and installed Victoriano Huerta and a government more favorable to business. He did this, it was claimed by President Wilson, without the authority or compliance of the U.S. government or any of its surrogates.

IN 1914 WOODROW WILSON invaded Veracruz. It was over the fact that a handful of American sailors had been taken from a U.S. ship, but, in fact, it was his desire to overthrow Huerta, destabilize his regime and encourage the rebels.

DURING THIS PERIOD, the price of oil per barrel doubled.

ACKNOWLEDGMENTS

I WISH TO THANK the publisher, Charlie Winton, for the literary opportunity. I also wish to thank Tracy Falco of Universal, for the filmic opportunity.

On a personal note: To Deirdre Stephanie and the late, great Brutarian . . . to G.G. and L.S. . . . to Charlie Cacique at the Agua Caliente Race Track, for the tip that led to Lazaro and so birthed this book . . . and finally, to my steadfast friend and ally, and a master at navigating the madness, Donald V. Allen.